THE
ROCK

A SULLIVAN AND BRODERICK
MURDER MYSTERY

ROBERT DAWS

urbanepublications.com

First published in Great Britain in 2017
by Urbane Publications Ltd
Suite 3, Brown Europe House, 33/34 Gleaming Wood Drive,
Chatham, Kent ME5 8RZ
Copyright © Robert Daws, 2017

A CIP catalogue record for this book is available
from the British Library.

ISBN 978-1-911331-19-3

Design and Typeset by Michelle Morgan

Cover by Michelle Morgan and Debbie at The Cover Collection

Printed and bound by CPI Group (UK) Ltd, Croydon, CR0 4YY

urbanepublications.com

FOR AMY, BETSY, MAY AND BEN

Can a father see his child

Weep, nor be with sorrow filled?

Can a mother sit and hear

An infant groan, an infant fear?

No, no! never can it be!

Never, never can it be!

William Blake

THE ROCK

GIBRALTAR 1966

THE CAPTAIN'S HOUSE stands proud above its high walls. From its imposing gates, statuesque lions gaze down impassively in reminiscence of its colonial past.

A lone Austin Cambridge moves past the front gates and continues down the dusty road, the silence of the afternoon broken only by the hum of its engine and the strains of Dave Brubeck's 'Take Five' floating from the nearby French windows of the house's large drawing room. To the east the garden rises in three terraces, finally ending at the base of the gigantic limestone Rock itself. To the west, the view crosses the town to the Straits of Gibraltar and the Moroccan coast of Africa. Below the surface of the narrow and busy seaway that separates these land masses, two mighty continents meet. But here on high ground, net curtains flutter in the breeze as a gramophone needle skips and jumps across deep black grooves.

The boy does not move, nor blink, as he stares at his reflection and his reflection stares back at him. For a moment, he no longer knows which is which. He needs to know. With huge effort he turns his head from the mirror and forces himself to look once more upon the carnage at the centre of the room.

A woman's hand hangs limply across the arm of a chaise longue - trickles of deep scarlet dried to the greying skin. Her blood stained boudoir robe is open, revealing a peach tinted silk charmeuse trouser set. The silk has risen up to the knee on one side, from which a bare calf, ankle and slender foot spread out in an act of petrified desperation. The glistening lipstick on her sumptuous lips belies the horror that shines through her bloodshot eyes. The steel handle of a knife protrudes from her chest, its sharpened tip buried deep within her heart.

A man steps in through the French window and surveys the scene. The fine lines of his tailored three-piece suit a sharp contrast to the chaos within the room. He turns and sees the boy trembling in a corner. The boy meets his stare and screams. Screams uncontrollably.

THE ROCK.
PRESENT DAY.

SHE SIGHED CONTENTEDLY as she stepped out through the French windows and onto the raised, tastefully decorated garden terrace. Free of the house and its darkened interior, the old lady took in the sights and smells of the perfectly manicured grounds. Even after all these years she never failed to smile when she stood on this spot. This she did every day, enjoying the delicate scent of breeze through the garden, the high westward easing sun beating down on the tall gates at the end of the driveway and the fluttering of the drawing room curtains in the warm summer air.

The radio played, barely audible, as the newsreader continued unperturbed. '...*Cross border delays are expected to increase even more from this Saturday the ninth of June, as major road works commence on the La Linea approach roads...*'

As she raised a glass of orange juice to her lips, a blood-curdling scream rang out from deep within the house. A blue rock thrush, momentarily perched on the terrace walls, took flight as the glass of orange fell from the the woman's mouth, smashing into sharp pieces at her feet.

She moved now, as fast as her ageing legs would carry her, back into the house and up to the first-floor landing. Another scream. She stood frozen to the spot, knowing that she must do something. But what?

She moved, more slowly now, to the bedroom door at the end of the upper hall and tapped gently upon it.

'Are you all right, dear?'

Silence. Another tap.

'Hello? Are you all right?'

Silence. Then the single click of the key turning in the lock. The heavy wooden door began to slowly creak open, revealing the terrible scene within. She could utter only four words.

'Oh... you poor thing.'

CHAPTER 1

THE VIOLENT THRUST of the aircraft's engines sent a disturbing vibration through the plane as it started to power its way down the runway of Luton's International Airport. Although she had experienced it a hundred times before, the outwardly composed thirty-one year old woman sitting in a window seat at the front of the passenger deck could not completely hide her anxiety. Nothing about the process of aviation seemed natural to her, and the grisly mental images from a dozen disaster movies were now running on a loop through her mind. This mental torture had not been helped by the five hour delay the passengers had been forced to endure due to strike action by French air traffic controllers. The vented frustration of some of her fellow flyers meant that the flight attendants had little good will to spare for a single woman travelling alone. She had tried smiling at the one male attendant on board, but had been as ruthlessly ignored by him as by his female colleagues.

The plane now started to rise and climb into the skies. A large and heavily perspiring man in the seat next to her gripped his arm rest and started to practise some kind of breathing technique obviously learnt for just such an occasion.

As the plane passed through the low lying cloud and moved higher into the blue, she finally felt relaxed enough to slip off her shoes and stretch her tense feet beneath the seat of the passenger in front. She once again opened the brightly pictured pages of the 'Guide to Gibraltar' that had been nestling in her lap. She had attempted this read so often over the previous weeks, that her failure to get beyond the opening two pages now made her smile rather than grimace. Somehow she had managed to glean that Gib was at the southern most tip of Europe and in places was covered in monkeys. Or were they apes? She also knew that it was not a lack of interest in the place itself that had created this casual response to study, more the circumstances that had led to her having to journey to Gibraltar in the first place. Visiting the Rock had not been a part of her grand plan. The job that she would have to endure for the next three months was a punishment. A barely concealed form of demotion. The hiding away of an embarrassing incident by an obsessively P.R. orientated, internationally renowned institution.

Tamara Sullivan once more gave up on the book in her hand. She leaned back in her seat, closed her eyes and prayed that the two and a half hour flight would bring less turbulence than the last few months of her life had managed to generate.

CHAPTER 2

THE WISTERIA ADORNING The Gibraltar Straits Hotel seemed to dance in the warm summer breeze. As the sun tipped its way over the western horizon and darkness filled the sky, a young couple sat on the hotel veranda sipping cocktails and gazing into each other's eyes. Both lovers were oblivious to the more mundane matters being concluded in the main conference room within.

'So once again, I would like to thank you for your time, energy and dedication, both tonight and hopefully on into the future. And before we all head home, it is my happy duty to announce that our joint small businesses initiative has succeeded in raising its target of twenty-five thousand pounds, thus enabling us to create, for Gibraltar's St. Margaret's Child Care Centre, a new play garden!'

The audience applauded warmly, and with some relief that the meeting was drawing to its long-overdue finish.

'Thank you, Mrs Jennifer Tavares, for all your hard work,' added the evening's master of ceremonies. 'Now, ladies and gentlemen, that will be all for this six monthly general meeting....' His words trailed off as he became aware that he was talking to over a hundred rear ends, all heading towards the main exit.

At the Atlantic Village Marina, moonlight glistened along the water's edge. Unlike the opulent yachts and apartment buildings that surrounded him, the lone motorcyclist preferred to keep to the shadows, his middle finger flicking the clutch as he waited impatiently.

Thirty yards away, in the darkened main cabin of one of the marina's finest vessels, his accomplice was hard at work with fevered intent. A hold-all bulged under the weight of its contents as the masked man took anything of obvious value and stuffed it inside. The yacht swayed and bowed on the water, as if trying to shake off its malevolent intruder. With a shrill, piercing screech, the yacht's alarm rang out as the man rushed back out onto the deck. The roar of the motorcycle engine was music to his ears as he jumped from the boat and clambered onto the back of the waiting bike. Clinging to his fellow rider for dear life, he tried to catch his breath as the bike took off at high speed. Seconds later, the two robbers passed effortlessly through the marina's open security gate as the guard in the booth shouted into his phone.

The bike leant heavily as it ate up the corner and sped down the marina road, which ran at a parallel with the airport's imposing runway. At this moment an Airbus A321 touched the ground, its engines exerting the huge power of reverse thrust which would finally bring it to a standstill. Simultaneously, the bike raced towards Sir Winston Churchill Avenue, the main road that crossed the runway and led to the Spanish border and the Costa del Sol beyond. The first indication that the robbers' timing was misjudged was a closed barrier prohibiting a crossing and the immediate possibility of an escape northward.

The tyres screeched in a sudden turn as its riders leant in hard and headed fast towards the centre of Gibraltar town.

Peering through the aircraft window as the plane neared touchdown on terra firma, Sullivan caught a glimpse of the fast moving motorcycle as it raced down the marina road. Her attention did not linger. Her eyes were drawn instead to the myriad lights of the sovereignty shining brightly against the pitch-black darkness of the Rock's vast backdrop.

The flight had mostly been spent trying to stop her fellow passenger chatting her up. The large man with the flying phobia seated next to her had insisted on transferring his fears into a constant stream of questions and banal observations. Worse still, he had begun to smell and the stench of drying perspiration was beginning to hang cloyingly in the air, despite the best efforts of the aircraft's noisy air conditioning system to disguise it. At one point, as they flew high over the outskirts of Madrid, she had even toyed with the idea of utilising her oxygen mask by way of escape. Fortunately, her companion had noticed the lack of warmth being returned by his beautiful co-passenger and had ceased conversation. However, as the plane began its descent to the peninsula, it became clear that his silence had been spent planning revenge.

'It's quite dangerous, you know,' he began once more, 'Landing in Gib. Fifth most dangerous airport in the world.'

'Goodness,' replied Sullivan.

'*The* number one, *numero uno* dangerous airport in the whole of Europe. It's the Rock, of course. Apparently causes dangerous up currents or down drafts, that sort of thing. And the runway is ridiculously short. Designed for military aircraft, you see. Pretty hairy most of the time. You religious at all?"

If she had bothered to answer, Sullivan might have told him that she was a Catholic. A lapsed Catholic with regular feelings of guilt about her wavering faith. Guilt, Sullivan had long ago decided, was something you had to get used to. Her religious failings moved to the back of an ever-growing queue of imperfections.

The aircraft reached the end of the runway and began to taxi towards the terminal - the sound of seat belts being prematurely unfastened signalled the start of the rush to get out of the claustrophobic tube. Sullivan chose to relax and wait for the mob to leave. Flying was no fun on a budget airline, and the rush to the baggage carousel was something she would pass on. After all, luggage handlers made all travellers equal by not serving up cases, prams and golf clubs on a first come first served basis. One got one's baggage as and when the fates allowed, and tonight Sullivan was cool with that. She was in no hurry to check into her budget hotel - merely short term accommodation until her apartment was available at the end of the week. There would also be nobody to meet her at the passenger terminal and Sullivan was cool with that too.

'Welcome to the Rock,' the flight attendant offered as Sullivan left the aircraft.

'Thanks,' she replied, 'but I'm not entirely sure I will be.'

Although evening, the narrow streets of Gibraltar Town were still busy with tourists. The speeding motorcycle weaved its way through them — its two riders growing increasingly anxious. This had not been their intended getaway route and as such was proving to be a haphazardly improvised Plan B. Rounding a corner, they narrowly missed a group of teenagers crossing the street - the exchange of insults between both parties broken only by the bike's angry acceleration up the street and away.

Minutes before, motorcycle officers Ferra and Bryant of the Royal Gibraltar Police Force had witnessed the robber's bike race past them. Within seconds, the policemen on their powerful Honda motorcycles were pursuing at speed – their duo of sirens giving clear indication that a chase was on.

Entering the densely packed Casement Square, alive with restaurants and promenaders, the thieves were forced to slow and manoeuvre through the thick throng of humankind. As they kicked and punched their way through, the shocked crowd parted like the Red Sea. No sooner had the parting closed, than it was forced open again to allow the flashing police motorcycles clearance. The younger revellers in the square laughed carelessly at the disruption. Older and wiser heads looked on in concern. A female tourist cried out in pain at the broken nose she had just received from the flailing fist of the passenger on the first motorcycle.

At last the felons broke free of the crowd and escaped down a narrow byway. Officers Ferra and Bryant followed just seconds behind, unfazed by the mayhem, their steely professionalism maintained in pursuit of their prey.

Jennifer and Martin Tavares had chosen to walk home from the hotel, stopping off at their favourite restaurant, Café Rojo, for a drink and some light supper. It had been a big night for Jennifer – the culmination of over a year's charity fundraising. Getting the much needed cash for the children's garden from local businesses had not been easy in difficult financial times. Martin looked at his handsome wife and felt the rush of pride and deep attraction he had always experienced in her company.

'That was a fantastic speech, Jennie. Really.'

The woman stopped dead in her tracks and turned to look at him.

'Are you feeling all right, Martin?'

'Uh... fine. Why?'

'Well, I might be mistaken, but that sounded like a compliment!'

Her man seemed almost hurt, but put his pride to one side as he looked into her eyes.

'I mean it. I'm very proud of you, Mrs Tavares.'

She smiled as her gaze moved to his lips, her body rising up on tiptoes as they kissed.

'Glad to see you're feeling charitable this evening,' Martin said, his cheeks reddening. As he leant in for a second kiss, his wife turned her head - distracted by the shrill sound of a fast approaching police siren. The road rumbled underfoot as a speeding motorcycle hurtled round the corner and headed straight for them.

'Jesus Christ!'

A second motorcycle with a police officer upon it passed at equal speed as the couple gasped in shock. Martin stepped away from his wife and out into the middle of the street.

'Bloody idiots! What the hell do you think you're doing?'

Then, to his horror, a third motorcycle appeared. The two-tone wailing of its siren deepened in pitch as the headlights doubled, tripled, quadrupled in size before the bike lurched heavily to its left, its plastic and metal scraping along the hard cobbled street. Martin dived to the ground to avoid being hit by the lethal machine. The police rider simultaneously fell from his seat a few yards further on. The now riderless motorcycle careered onwards across the street, smashing into a grocery store shop front at terrifying speed.

In a daze, Martin pulled himself to his feet and moved slowly towards the mangled wreckage of plastic and metal.

'Jennifer? Jennie!' Martin shouted as he reached the shop front. Beside the crashed motorcycle, his wife lay prostrate and lifeless, her neck bent at a most horrific angle. Her long blonde hair clotted with red caught and tangled in the gears of the motorcycle. Martin tried to speak, to move forward and help, but his limbs seemed paralysed. He stood helpless and alone, his mind racing in an attempt to take in the enormity and shock of the scene before him. For what seemed like an eternity, Martin stood motionless – a calm before the storm of emotions that would inevitably rip free with horrific force. At last, the sound of footsteps behind him. Police Officer Gavin Bryant's dishevelled form appeared at his side. Martin's voice betrayed no emotion as he turned his head to look at the blood-spattered face of the man responsible for this living hell.

'What have you done? What have you done to her?'

CHAPTER 3

THE FLOOR OF the A&E Department at Gibraltar's centrally located hospital felt harder underfoot than usual. Swing doors clattered open as the paramedics swept Jennifer's stretcher down the corridor like an Olympic bob-sleigh team, Martin Tavares and two police officers following closely behind.

'The RTA from the town, Dr Budrani.' The young paramedic spoke clearly, but with a tangible air of panic in her voice.

'Get her straight through to theatre,' replied Budrani, following the paramedic as she continued to call out Jennifer's BP stats.

Martin Tavares was once again in a trance-like state. His anguish had exploded back at the scene of the accident. Seeing his wife's limp body being lifted into the ambulance, Tavares had punched out at Bryant, the forlorn traffic cop. Only the combined efforts of the newly arrived police officers and several bystanders had prevented him from adding to the night's casualty list.

'Martin?' The porter's voice pulled him out of his trance.

'David.'

'Are you okay? What's happened?' David asked, registering the anguish on Martin's face. 'It's Jennie. She... she's...'

The hospital porter stood silent for a moment, allowing the meaning of this to set in.

'Oh God. Oh no.'

The swing-doors were once again pushed apart as the fleeing porter ran down the corridor and into the operating theatre.

'Jennie? Jennie, it's me. It's David.'

'I'm sorry,' Dr Budrani said sternly, 'but you'll have to leave. We may have to operate.'

'But I have to be here!' he replied. 'Save her! Please! She's my sister!'

The old lady sat alone in the darkened room. The ancestral faces that stared down at her from the ancient paintings upon its walls all seemed to share the same expression. It was one she recognised whenever she glimpsed her own face in the mirror. A slight aloofness that could not conceal an anxiety that played around the eyes and mouth. It was, she had persuaded herself, only imagination – her own fears transferred to the images caught in fading paint upon cracking canvas.

As much as the afternoon sun brought her happiness, so the deep swallowing darkness of night brought her fearful and tormented nightmares. The house, so old and so long a part of her family, was not a home but a shell in which her last days would slowly be eked out. She tried again and again to remember the brighter times with husband and friends filling the rooms with life and laughter. But each image, each memory, would fade as quickly as it had appeared. All those times. All that love and warmth was gone now. Long gone.

The old lady sat alone in the darkened room and waited – waited for the demon above to rise and engulf her in pain.

In a private room off one of the main wards of the hospital, PC Gavin Bryant sat up in bed, his head pounding beneath a blood-stained gauze. The tap at the door signalled the arrival of his superior officer, Chief Superintendent Harriet Massetti.

'How are you doing, Bryant?' Massetti asked with as much warmth as she could muster.

'Just a few bruises, ma'am. They're keeping me in for observation.'

Massetti said nothing; just gave a slight smile and a nod of the head.

'I didn't stand a chance. I was in pursuit, turned the corner and there he was... just standing in the middle of the road.'

'I understand,' replied Massetti. Whether or not she really did was not entirely clear.

'I swear. I didn't even see her standing there!'

'Understood, constable. You just, er... just get yourself together. All right?'

Massetti backed towards the door. Although nothing had been said, Bryant knew something was troubling her.

'She... they brought her here as well, didn't they? The woman, I mean.'

'Yes.'

Bryant hesitated for a moment, not sure that he really wanted to hear the answer.

'And?'

'I'm afraid she didn't make it, Bryant.'

Only two words escaped Bryant's lips: 'Oh God.'

'I've tried to speak to the husband downstairs, but... for obvious reasons... it's not the appropriate time. Just try and keep it together, constable. We'll sort this.'

Bryant lay back, his eyes fixed on the ceiling above him. It was a tragic accident. It wasn't his fault. He knew that he had to stay strong. A single tear slid down his cheek. He quickly wiped it away and turned to bury his face in his pillow.

Accompanied by two constables, C S Massetti headed for the main hospital exit. She seemed tiny next to her companions. Her dark, short-cropped hair revealed a delicate, finely featured bone structure that her distant Genoese ancestors would have recognised as their own. Yet any serving officer of the RGP would quickly confirm that Massetti's outward feminine charms hid a ruthless and powerful professional will of steel. These characteristics were about to be challenged. She and her constables had barely reached reception when they were halted in their tracks by a group of local press reporters, all eager for a story.

'Chief Superintendent Massetti? This is the second accident involving police vehicles from your force in the last twelve months. Would you say your drivers are reckless?'

Massetti kept a calm exterior, despite the anger that was building inside her.

'Our drivers are highly trained professionals. This is a tragic accident brought about by the reckless driving of mindless criminals. My officer, PC Bryant, is being treated here for minor injuries and shock. I wish to send my sincere condolences to Mr Tavares and his family at this difficult time. I will make a full statement regarding this incident later today. Thank you.'

Sensing her unease, the constables stepped to Massetti's side and escorted her to the waiting car. Although the reporters had begun to follow, they were distracted by the sight of Martin Tavares and his brother-in-law leaving the main building.

Both were visibly pale and shaken. David took a written statement from Martin's hand and began to read, his voice cracking under the strain of grief.

'Words cannot express the deep despair that my brother-in-law Martin, myself and the rest of my sister's family feel today. Her death should not have happened, but…'

'The police are supposed to be here to protect us, not take our lives!' Martin exploded, the spittle flying from his lips. 'Someone has to pay for this! I will not rest until they are forced to pay!'

The slamming of car doors drew attention to the police vehicle parked just a few metres away. Looking over, Martin locked eyes with Massetti seated in the back of the car. Pushing his way through the reporters, Martin moved towards her.

'You! You killed her! You killed my wife!'

Before he could reach the visibly shaken Chief Superintendent, the police vehicle was driven away. Massetti sat back in her seat - her head throbbing. This was not the manner in which she wished to see this incident proceed.

CHAPTER 4

SULLIVAN MOVED THROUGH the reception area of the hotel. She was not due to report to Police HQ until ten, so had decided to spend an hour strolling through the centre of Gibraltar Town. Being unaccustomed to hotel living, she had decided to make the most of her week's stay in the pleasant three star, centrally-located Hotel Alameda. Since she had expected only budget type accommodation — things were momentarily looking up. Treating herself to a brandy nightcap in the hotel bar the night before, she had successfully fended off the inebriated advances of a travelling salesman and, for the first time in months, slept like a baby in her deluxe double room. The next morning she had even allowed herself the indulgence of a continental breakfast, delivered to her room on the dot of seven-thirty and eaten with relish as she viewed the news headlines on Sky.

Picking up a tourist map from the concierge desk, Sullivan exited the main doors and hit the street. As she moved from the gentle chill of the hotel's air-conditioned lobby, the heat outside almost knocked her off her feet. It wasn't even nine o'clock. She could only imagine what the temperature would achieve by midday and then onwards through a baking afternoon. She had a sun hat in her bag to protect her pale skin, but chose not to put it on - she didn't want to arrive with 'bed head' on her first day with the Royal Gibraltar Police Force. Better instead to keep to the shade and trust in her 'SF thirty' sun protection lotion.

Turning right into the alarmingly named Bomb House Lane, she passed the Gibraltar Museum on her left. Deciding that the ancient Moorish baths within could wait for another day, she headed on towards Main Street. She could sense that the heart of Gibraltar was beginning to beat. Down the network of myriad little lanes, shops were opening for the day. The general bustle of local people hurrying to work and the smell of fresh coffee and exotic breads from the many little cafes along the way excited Sullivan. It felt in many ways as though it was the first day of a holiday, and even as she turned onto Main Street to be confronted by the familiar shop frontage of a Marks and Spencer store, she knew she could be nowhere other than the Mediterranean.

Her allotted hour was passing swiftly as she browsed the smaller shops and strolled along the many narrow passageways. A tiny pavement cafe finally stopped her in her tracks, enticing her in for a first 'cafe con leche' of the day and a moment of contemplation. She was aware that she was far more relaxed than she should be on a first day of a new job. The contrast of place and atmosphere were playing their part. Months spent under investigation by her own kind had left her scarred and emotionally battered. She had survived, but only just. Being cleared, but not exonerated, of the charge of professional misconduct meant that she had no choice but to disappear from the Met and begin again. All her plans, hopes and ambitions had come to nothing. But here, drinking strong coffee in a foreign but familiar land, she felt a strange feeling of freedom.

As the first cruise ship tourists began to populate the lanes around her, Sullivan paid the waiter and hailed a cab to take her downtown to begin her new life.

The sign on the front of the Royal Gibraltar Police Headquarters glistened in the mid-morning sun as Sullivan's taxi pulled up at the front of the grey stone building. Before her, a central archway led to a set of iron gates, through which Sullivan could see a large courtyard busy with police officers. Further along to her right, was the single-doored reception entrance for public enquiries. Instead of heading for either of these front entrances, Sullivan moved to the side of the building in search of a doorway for police personnel only. A passing motorcyclist wolf-whistled as he passed her. Sullivan was used to this - even at work. She had long been admired by her colleagues for her hard work and tenacity, but her striking figure and long dark hair had also found many admirers. At five foot nine and a half inches tall, she often found herself standing eye-to-eye with her male colleagues. Much to their annoyance, she was able to outrun and out punch a good many of them too. Being single, she tended not to mention these last attributes on a first date. Her former Chief Inspector had nicknamed her the 'Colleen'. At the time it had been meant affectionately. It was an affection that had worn impossibly thin during her last few months with the Met. The nickname, however, had stuck.

'You all right, Miss?' asked one of two passing constables.

'Sorry?'

'If you're looking for a policeman, you've found him,' the constable replied.

'I'm just looking for a way into the building, thank you very much.'

'No access through here, I'm afraid. Police personnel only. I can... uh... take you round the front, if you like?'

Whether or not the innuendo had been intended, was not entirely clear.

'That won't be necessary,' Sullivan replied as she pushed her hand inside her jacket, extracting a warrant card. 'I can sort myself out, thank you, constable.'

'Ah. Er, yes, Sarge. Just straight on round,' the young man replied with a weak smile.

Sullivan moved on to the station's side entrance, stopped for a moment to compose herself and then strode purposefully into the building. Holiday over.

The door clicked open and Massetti entered her office.

'It's a damned bloody mess, Aldarino. That's what it is.'

Sergeant Aldarino decided not to confirm his boss's negative appraisal of the situation. After nearly ten years at Masetti's side, he knew this was by far the best approach. Especially when he had negative news of his own to impart.

'The Commissioner's telephoned, ma'am. He's returning from his holiday straight away.'

'Yeah, I bet he is,' Massetti replied curtly.

She sat at her desk, the pile of pending paperwork upon it only darkening her mood. Alderino continued.

'And, uh, television and radio have been on. They want a statement from someone.'

'I'll need time to draft something. Tell them they'll have it by lunchtime and get that report from the crash site as soon as possible, will you, Aldarino?'

'Well it's a bit early for...'

'Just get me the basics, all right? And please, God, let it be as Bryant and Ferra said it was. The last thing we need is this incident spiralling into a public relations nightmare.'

'Yes, ma'am. Oh and, ma'am?'

'Yes, Sergeant?'

'DS Sullivan is here.'

'Who?'

'The new Met officer on secondment. Arrived from London last night.'

'Ah.'

Alderino could see that she was still none the wiser.

'I briefed you last week, ma'am. You said to…'

'Yes, yes, all right, Aldarino. I have had a lot on my mind.'

Aldarino nodded and left the room, leaving Massetti a few minutes in which to stew, before once more tapping upon the door with another list of urgent matters and dates for her itinerary. Not for the first time and certainly not for the last, Aldarino thanked his lucky stars that he had chosen to remain a sergeant.

The old lady bent to pick up the basket of damp washing on the floor of the kitchen. She would now carry out the familiar job of drying and ironing the clothes that were in it. It was a task she found increasingly difficult to perform - her mobility recently becoming so much more limited with the pain from her arthritic hip joints. If only Maria had been able to stay. For twenty-five years her housekeeper had effortlessly taken the weight of household chores away from her mistress.

But the old lady had had to let her go. She would not have understood the changed priorities within the household and the very particular demands of the person who now occupied the upstairs bedroom of the house with its view of the upper garden and the Rock. Maria would have wanted to help. To care and ease her mistress's burden. But the old lady could not allow that. What possessed the house now could only be exorcised by herself, and herself alone. It was her duty. A guilt that had to be assuaged.

The old lady moved slowly across the kitchen - the basket of washed clothes in her hands. She had to get them dried and ironed to perfection. The punishment for not doing so would be too much to bear.

'So, you're with us for three months then, Sullivan.' Massetti peered over her desk at the female officer in front of her.

'Yes, ma'am. I'm very much looking forward to it.'

Masetti knew this to be a lie, and made a mental note to make sure that it wouldn't be the first of many.

'The last one that came over here from the Met was supposed to have 'enhanced relationship and liaison mechanisms' between our two forces. At least that's what the blurb said. By the time he left, I can't say I'd spotted much enhancement — though there had been a couple of liaisons. Perhaps your reason for being here is a little less ambitious...?'

'I'm just here to observe, assist and advise, ma'am.'

'Ye-es. There's a lot of observing and advising going on these days. Not much of it seems to be of assistance, though.'

'Well, I hope I may prove to be of some use to you, ma'am.'

'Indeed. From what I've read of your record, Detective Sergeant, we may be the ones proving useful to you.' Massetti hadn't wanted to set this tone, but it had been a rough morning and she wasn't in the mood for niceties.

'I very much hope there'll be some mutual benefit gained during my stay here, ma'am.'

'I'll insist upon it, Sullivan. If you think you're just going to be mooching around like a United Nations observer, you'll be sadly mistaken. I've decided that the best way you can observe is to serve. You're a police officer and therefore you should be doing police work. You can conclude what you like after you've finished here. As it happens, we're temporarily short of a detective sergeant in CID, so as far as I'm concerned you're the man. If you have any complaints, you can bleat back to your bosses in the Met. Understood?'

'Perfectly, ma'am.'

'You'll be joining Chief Inspector Broderick's team. He should make your stay on the Rock quite an interesting one.'

Before Sullivan could enquire further about her new mentor, a tap at the door interrupted proceedings. Sergeant Aldarino poked his head around the doorframe.

'Sorry, ma'am. You're needed.'

'Very well,' Massetti replied. 'Get someone to escort DS Sullivan here to the third floor, will you?'

Both women stood. Massetti felt a sudden twinge of guilt at her welcoming brief.

'Er.. settled into your digs alright, have you?'

'Actually, ma'am, I won't get into my apartment till the weekend. I'm staying at the Alameda 'til then.'

'How very pleasant for you.'

'Yes, ma'am.'

'Look, we're a tight, loyal and highly professional force here on the Rock. A very different scale of operation to the one you've been used to. But if you keep your head down and do the work, you could find you've gone a long way to digging yourself out of the hole you've made for yourself. No te descatilles. Don't step out of line. Understood?'

'Perfectly.'

'Good luck, then.'

'Will I need it, ma'am?'

'I'd say that's for you to find out and me to observe, Sullivan. That'll be all.'

CHAPTER 5

SERGEANT ALDARINO HAD decided against calling another officer to guide their latest visitor to CID. At a fast pace, he led the way himself.

'It's a bit of a maze, but you'll soon get used to it. Old buildings have their charms, but order and convenience are not among them.'

Sullivan had instinctively taken a liking to the tall, grey haired Gibraltarian. He was the only policeman who'd bothered to smile at her for as long as she could remember. They continued along a narrow corridor and then climbed a stone staircase to the floor above. Sullivan had by now deduced that the Police HQ was basically a two-storey building surrounding a large quadrangle. Very different in feel and lay-out to anything she had known in the UK. To her great surprise, she felt immediately at home.

Now on the first floor, Aldarino led her down a long corridor occupied by several offices partitioned off by walls of frosted glass. Eventually the sergeant stopped outside an anonymous door, second from the end.

'Here's where you live. By the way, don't be put off by the Chief Super's manner. She's having a bad morning. She's the best of them here. I've been with her a decade now and I wouldn't want to work for anyone else. She'll play fair by you, if you play fair by her.'

A pager attached to the sergeant's tunic began to bleep.

'Talking of the devil. Me voy a dar el bote. I'll be off.' He nodded towards the door. 'You can make your own introductions. They'll be expecting you.'

Turning his pager off, the sergeant headed briskly back down the corridor. Sullivan turned, gave the door a cursory tap and entered. The small office was cramped. Too cramped for the four desks and many filing cabinets that met her eye. A single large window looked out across the dry docks and the sea opposite. There was only one inhabitant. A single officer sat with his back to the door - his focus firmly on the computer screen in front of him.

'Sir?' Sullivan said. The man did not bother to respond. 'Sir? DS Sullivan. Just arrived from London. Chief Superintendent Massetti tells me I'll be working with you.'

'Nope,' the man replied, still refusing to be distracted from his work.

'Oh. There must be some mistake...'

'And you just made it, Sarge,' said the man, as he finally spun round to face her. His youthful looks suggested to Sullivan that this was not her boss.

'Whoa!' the man involuntarily let slip at the sight of his new and attractive colleague.

'I beg your pardon?' replied Sullivan coldly.

'I meant... hello, Sarge. I'm DC Calbot.'

Sullivan raised an eyebrow, by way of suggesting to the detective constable that he might consider standing in the presence of a senior officer. The expression was quickly interpreted, and Calbot jumped to his feet.

'Completely forgot you were turning up today.'

'So it would appear,' Sullivan responded. 'And Chief Inspector Broderick?'

'Ah, yeah, sorry. Guv's not here.'

'I see. When will he be back?'

'Tomorrow. Dentist,' Calbot replied, in his trademark staccato manner.

'Tomorrow?' Sullivan questioned incredulously. 'Abscess. Right at the back.'

'Sounds painful.'

'Let's hope so, eh?'

'I beg your pardon?' Sullivan responded, once more uneasy with Calbot's disrespectful tone.

'Joke.' Calbot grinned. 'Just a joke, Sarge.'

Sullivan's blank expression told the DC that she had no intention of sharing it.

The acrid smoke swirled around Martin Tavares's nostrils as the ash grew longer at the tip of his half spent cigarette. His free hand gripped the armchair as if it were a long-lost friend.

The home he had shared with Jennie all their married life was now full of well-meaning, but interfering relatives and friends – all hoping to be helpful. Martin barely registered their presence. He didn't want help: he wanted Jennifer back. The hushed whispers of the assembled body faded as his concentration was drawn towards the monotonous ticking of the clock on the far wall, its hands showing a quarter to three. For a fleeting moment, he found solace in its stability; its rhythmic continuity. Time would never fade. It could never die or be extinguished. It would always be there, moving forward, expanding. Time didn't come to an end - only life did. He knew Jennie would not have agreed. She had her faith. Her belief in the continuation of the spirit and soul. But soon she would be nothing more than burnt ashes and a ghost in a thousand grief-filled, haunted dreams. Two people died that night, Martin thought. If there was a God, he hoped Jennie had found her heaven, because one thing was certain – he had found hell.

Sullivan was unsure of what to make of Calbot. His laid back demeanour seemed to her to be 'affected'. A little too worked at to utterly convince. He was certainly easy on the eye, although very far from being her type. Too young for a start, and far too cocky. Too much like a lot of young coppers, she thought - gobby and overly styled. Male estate agents seemed to suffer from a similar kind of self-presentation. All gelled hair and trimmed stubble above the waterline. All desperate paddling and no underpants beneath. He had some charm, so she wouldn't completely write him off. Not yet anyway.

'So, you're being chucked in at the deep end are you?' Calbot ventured.

'Meaning what, exactly?' Sullivan bridled once more at Calbot's inappropriate question.

'Massetti's smelt some cheap labour. You're filling in while DS Marquez is off with glandular.'

'Glandular?' Sullivan queried.

'Fever. Second time in a year. Wiped him out completely.'

'This department does seem to have more than its fair share of painful medical conditions. I trust you're not likely to collapse with anything soon?'

'No, Sarge. I'm well fit.'

'Any chance of bringing me up to speed with your present case work?' Sullivan asked, changing the subject. Calbot grabbed the uppermost file from his desk and handed it to her.

'This one's fresh. Boat mechanic down at the West Marina accidentally dropped a boat on his wife's head. Guv's not completely convinced it was, though.'

'Was what? A boat?'

'No, an accident. Awaiting forensics.'

'Aren't we always?' Sullivan began to sift through the file. 'This is a bit chaotic, isn't it?'

'Yeah, not his strong point, paperwork,' Calbot replied.

Sullivan glanced at the huge mess of papers on Calbot's desk.

'Nor yours, by the look of things.'

Calbot smirked as though Sullivan had just given him a compliment. 'That last bloke they sent over from your lot... nice guy. Bolton, wasn't it? Lawrence Bolton?'

'No idea.'

'Not that we saw much of him. We reckoned he thought he was on a bit of a holiday.'

'Really?'

'Left the Force altogether. Does security now, up in Marbella. Earns three times what he was picking up as a copper. At least that's what we heard...'

'Then you've probably heard quite enough,' Sullivan replied, aware that she was losing her patience.

'You can never hear enough, Sarge. Not in this job.'

Sullivan's eyes narrowed. Aware of an incoming reprimand, Calbot responded with a huge grin. The flash of the young man's cosmetically whitened teeth, stopped Sullivan in her tracks.

'Fancy a coffee?' Calbot beamed. 'My treat.'

The ice cold water cascaded over his body as he stared unceasingly at the small black mark on the cream tiles. The sound of trickling water had deepened Martin's trance-like state. He barely registered the voice which came, muffled but insistent, through the bathroom door.

'Martin? It's David. Are you all right?'

David had been on some sort of suicide watch since leaving the hospital. He had not consciously admitted this to himself, but that's what his constant monitoring of Martin amounted to. As a voluntary hospital porter, he had seen trauma and grief many times before and could spot the signs of imminent self-harming well in advance. Concentrating on his brother-in-law had stopped him from drowning in a sea of his own grief. His beautiful sister - his kind, funny and ever present sister was now lying cold within the hospital's morgue. That same morgue to which he had pushed so many hundreds of dead bodies over the years. He could feel the pain and anger rising inside him. He must keep control. Concentrate on the living. Care and protect the living.

'Martin? It's me. Please let me know that you're all right.'

CHAPTER 6

THE CLANGING OF metallic trays against the recesses in the counter did nothing to help Ferra's headache that morning. The police canteen in which he and Bryant were queuing had been recently refurbished and a new 'self-service' regime instigated. The new decor was an obvious pastiche of Starbucks, but sadly, the opportunity for its customers to serve themselves with any speed or efficiency was being undermined by the painfully slow cashier at the end of the line. The food and coffee were of a better standard though, but then the rise in quality had also meant a hike in prices. But if you didn't pack yourself a sandwich — and a number of officers didn't, wouldn't or couldn't — then there was little else by way of convenient choice.

'Three-nil tonight, I reckon,' Calbot offered his colleagues as he joined the line and reached for a ham and cheese sandwich.

'Two-one,' Bryant replied.

'Nah, no chance they'll score. Two-nil, maybe.'

'Both goals Berbatov?'

'Oh yeah. What do you reckon, Ferra?'

'Not a whole lot, really,' the officer replied. 'Not been keeping up with it. I still reckon Porto for the cup, though.'

Calbot pulled a face. 'I reckon you need to start watching golf, mate.'

'Don't want to die in my sleep, mate.'

The men laughed and moved a little further along the line, picking up soft drinks along the way. Calbot took his opportunity...

'I know you two have been temporarily suspended. That's just shit.'

'Due process,' Ferra replied, shrugging his shoulders. 'That's why we're in today. They know it wasn't our fault. Doesn't stop them making us feel as if it was, though.'

'You both okay?' Calbot asked.

Bryant looked him straight in the eye. 'Been better.'

'Yeah, well. Not your fault. That's clear as day. Tough on you though.'

His colleagues nodded. There was an awkward pause.

'Actually, I'll grab this lot later.' Calbot looked across to the cashier. 'You could stand here all day waiting for her to get your change right. Catch you tonight. I owe you both a pint.'

'Tell us about it,' Ferra called after him. 'We were thinking you'd had your pockets sewn up.'

Calbot entered the office to find Sullivan still rifling through the files - a mountain of 'seen' and 'to-see' on either side of her.

'Sorry, no coffee. The queue was running out of the building.'

'That's okay.'

'How're you getting on?' he asked.

Sullivan barely raised her eyes from the files, trying to keep conversation to a minimum.

'Fine.'

'Fancy seeing a corpse?' Calbot asked, reaching for his mobile phone.

'A corpse?'

'The boat mechanic's wife. Thought a trip to pathology might break your morning up a bit.'

'Well, put so sweetly, how could a girl refuse?'

Sullivan was up and out of the door before Calbot could compose a retort.

The pair made their way through the hospital's main reception, avoiding the lifts in favour of the stairs.

'She was flat as a pancake when we got to her,' Calbot said, finishing off the ham panini he had stopped off for on the way to St. Bernards.

'What?'

'Well, not completely flat, but... well, you'll see. Never seen anything like it myself.'

They headed down to the basement level, through double doors and into a long corridor with many other corridors running off it. Calbot strode on as Sullivan followed.

'It's a maze down here,' Calbot told her. 'You'll get used to it though.'

'Pathology departments always seem to be hidden away,' Sullivan observed.

'That's because it's the last department anyone wants to have to find. Most of the people who come down here don't come back up again. Not right away, anyhow.'

The pathology department located, Calbot and Sullivan pushed the double doors aside and entered. On the right was the door to a consulting room. There was a name upon it: Prof. Gerald Laytham. Calbot tapped and entered straight away.

Standing at his desk was a tall, avuncular looking man in his mid-fifties. Calbot breezily made introductions.

'Morning, Professor Laytham. This is DS Sullivan. On secondment from the Met.'

The professor held out his hand in greeting. Sullivan shook it and smiled.

'Pleased to meet you, Sullivan. I'm fairly new here myself. Welcome, I suppose. Shall we visit the dead?'

Laytham led the two detectives out of his office and across the corridor to the pathology theatre. The large, cold and austere space had a covered corpse on an examining table at its centre.

'Not much I can offer you, I'm afraid,' Laytham remarked, as he peeled back the cover to reveal the wildly distorted shape of what was once a middle-aged woman. 'Mrs Bassano's death was instantaneous, there's no doubt about that. Multiple internal organ rupture, haemorrhaging, you name it. The weight of the boat, plus gravity, and you can imagine what happened. Like stamping on a balloon full of water, really.'

'Thanks for that, Prof,' Calbot replied, his ham panini beginning to trouble him.

The viewing over, Calbot and Sullivan made their way back towards the unmarked police car parked outside the hospital.

A dog started to bark and Sullivan looked around to see where the sound was coming from. Calbot checked his mobile and the barking stopped. *How irritating,* Sullivan thought, *to be caught out by a ringtone.*

'It's Broderick.' Calbot smiled smugly and spoke into his iPhone.

'Hi, Guv. Laytham just confirmed Mrs Bassano's cause of death. Where are you now? What? I can't make you out. Where?'

The line went dead. It was Calbot's turn to be irritated. 'Bollocks.'

'What did he say?' Sullivan asked.

'Dunno. Couldn't understand a word he was yelling at me. Oh, except one that is. How do you fancy a trip to the waterfront?'

Sullivan had already decided that, for today at least, Calbot could lead and she would follow.

CHAPTER 7

THE TWO DETECTIVES drove along Rosia Road, turning off into a maze of industrial units leading down to the water's edge. Amongst them stood an older building with a large sign announcing marine engineering services. Back in the eighties when the site was being redeveloped, a preservation order had been slapped on it just days before it was to be pulled down. Although no beauty, it was certainly an eccentric-looking building, complete with ample living quarters above the vast catacomb of the building itself.

As they approached, Sullivan and Calbot saw an old Mercedes estate parked at an alarming angle on the hard standing at the front.

'Brace yourself,' Calbot said, nodding in the direction of the Mercedes. 'That's the guv'nor's car.'

Parking up, the two walked towards the open doors which led to the inside of the large building. Just yards from the doors, Sullivan spoke.

'Don't look now, but there's someone watching us.'

Calbot scanned the vicinity. 'What? Where?'

'First floor window. Behind the net curtain.'

Calbot looked straight up at the window, catching a glimpse of a hand as it retreated behind the curtains. Sullivan looked at the Detective Constable with disapproval.

'I hope you don't respond to all orders in that way, Calbot?'

'You what, Sarge?'

'I said, *don't* look.'

'Oh…yeah…soz,' Calbot mumbled as Sullivan led the way into the building.

The cavernous, dimly lit interior revealed a large area at its centre that had been cordoned off with police tape. A hydraulic boat lift rose from the decking within the space - a fifteen-foot motor launch attached to it. Although she had little doubt that it presented no danger, the whole set-up looked fairly precarious to Sullivan. Suddenly, from behind the boat, a middle-aged man appeared, wearing old overalls.

'If this is your boss, tell him to stop. Stop now!' the man yelled, pointing in the direction of the lift's control panel. As he spoke, the hydraulic lift sprang to life, the boat dropping a couple of feet in nanoseconds, causing Calbot and Sullivan to spring back in surprise.

Walking briskly around to where they had been directed, Sullivan could see a somewhat dishevelled looking man standing at the controls. He seemed unsure of how to work them. Eventually he gave up, switched off the controls and glanced over towards them. Sullivan had assumed, even before spotting the heavy swelling on the side of the man's face, that this was Chief Inspector Broderick. He was clearly in is late forties, well built and bullish looking. Brown hair, peppered with grey and a slightly receding hairline, topped a well tanned and slightly ruddy face. He was certainly better looking than Sullivan had expected. He was also very bad tempered. This came as no surprise to her.

'Bruddy thing!' Broderick cursed, dismounting from the machine.

'It's a skill, you know,' the man in overalls barked. 'You can't just turn up and expect to be able to work a machine like that.'

Ignoring his words, Broderick walked towards the new arrivals and nodded at Sullivan. 'Who's vis?'

'I'm DS Sullivan, Chief Inspector. Pleased to meet you.'

'Yoo noo?'

'Officer on secondment, sir, yes. From London.' Broderick shook his head. 'Norody bruddy tells me anything!'

'What did he say?' Calbot asked, as Broderick moved off towards the front of the boat house.

'He said, nobody tells him anything. I think the anaesthetic is impeding his speech.'

Calbot smirked, 'Oh dear. What a shame.'

'For me, yeah.' Sullivan sighed. 'Great start, eh? Just brilliant.'

Outside, Broderick sat in his Mercedes, scribbling furiously in a brown leather-bound notebook. The man in overalls stood beside him. He looked up as Sullivan and Calbot exited from the shadows of the building into the fierce heat of the sun.

'What is this all about?' the man asked, raising his arms in the air.

'I sloddin 'ell giv 'ub,' the Chief Inspector growled, tearing a page from his notebook and handing it to the man. The man looked at it in confusion.

'Do you sell fish?' he read out loud and turned to Sullivan. 'What the hell does this mean?'

'The, uh... Chief Inspector asked,' Sullivan replied, attempting translation, 'Whether or not you sell fish, Mr...?'

'Bessano. It was my wife who died here.'

'I'm sorry, Mr Bessano.'

Broderick interrupted. 'Yust onsor the gestion, pwees.'

'Sell fish? No, I mend boats. If you want fish you'll need to go to the market.'

Broderick furiously scribbled another note and this time thrust the pad at Sullivan.

'The Inspector asks if you can recommend anyone. For fish, I imagine.'

'Oh. Well, Medina Bros at the market is probably your best bet. Second counter on the left. What does this have to do with the death of my wife, exactly?'

More scribbling, followed by another thrust of the notepad towards Sullivan.

'The Chief Inspector says: *Nothing. I just like good fish.*'

A few moments' confused silence followed. Sullivan decided to change the conversation. 'Is there anyone else staying here, Mr Bassano?'

'No, not really,' Bassano replied, clearly taken aback.

'Is that right?' Sullivan queried. 'Only I thought I saw somebody upstairs when we arrived, sir.'

'Oh. Yes. Of course. That is my grandson. He's been here for a few days while his parents are in Portugal. They're hurrying back now, of course, after the news.'

'Was he here yesterday?' Calbot asked. 'During all that?'

'Yes, he was. He's very upset, I'm sure you understand.'

Broderick scribbled another note. It read: *'Call him'.*

'Please,' Sullivan added under her breath. 'Would you mind calling him down, sir? We'd just like to have a little chat. Nothing scary, I promise.'

Bassano hesitated for a moment, then began to call. 'Julio! Julio, come down here, please!'

The clearly nervous boy appeared at the upstairs window, his eyes stained red.

Broderick led the way back into the building. The others followed, with Bassano still clearly upset at the request to see his grandson.

'Look, how many times?' Bassano pleaded. 'It was an accident! Julia had brought me tea. I thought she had gone. I lowered the boat. It dropped, like you saw. It's a fault with the lift, it must be — it's never happened before. It just dropped. I don't know why she was even under the boat!'

Broderick threw Sullivan a look as if to say that he'd be interested to discover the reason for that himself.

'Why can't you just leave us in peace?' Bassano continued. 'We've had enough grief this past twenty-four hours.'

Julio appeared at his grandfather's side. Sullivan looked at the clearly traumatised boy and smiled gently.

'Right. Julio. We are police officers. There's no need to be afraid. We just need to ask you a few questions. Is that OK?'

The child looked at Bassano for approval.

'Look, leave the lad alone,' the grandfather said. 'Can't you see he's upset enough as it is?'

'I'm sorry, Mr Bassano, but we really do need to get to the bottom of this. Do you like boats, Julio?' Sullivan asked gently.

The child looked at his grandfather, then nodded his head.

Sullivan continued, 'They're great, aren't they?'

Another nod.

'Is that boat your favourite?' Sullivan pointed to the boat. Another nod.

'Does your grandfather let you get inside the boat sometimes, Julio?'

'Now, that's quite enough,' Bassano barked. 'This is getting ridiculous. He is terrified. Escamao!'

Calbot placed a reassuring hand on Bassano's shoulder. The grandfather's reaction had alerted Sullivan to another possibility. She continued her probing under Broderick's silent stare.

'Have you ever tried to drive a boat on your own, Julio?'

Reluctantly, the boy nodded his head.

'Is that what you were doing yesterday?'

'What the hell are you saying?' Bassano cried. 'You've no right to interrogate him like this! He's just a boy!'

Chief Inspector Broderick touched Sullivan on the arm and indicated that she should wait. He moved swiftly to the hydraulic's controls. On the floor where they had fallen lay a large bag of sweets. Holding them up for all to see he asked as best he could... 'Dese are 'oors ah vey, Oolio?'

'What do you mean?' Bassano replied.

Broderick looked to his translator for help. Sullivan nodded to him and turned once more to the boy.

'Those are your sweets, aren't they, Julio?'

The boy looked again to his grandfather but could take no more. Tears began to fall down his cheeks once more. Bassano swept the lad into his arms and then turned on the accusers in desperation.

'Okay, okay! Listen. It wasn't his fault. Please. He came down here on his own. He's done it before — to play on the boat. We tried telling him time and time again to keep away.

Julia told me she was going to find him. She must have been trying to catch him when it happened. Maybe that was why she was under the boat, I don't know. Next thing, I heard a cry and came running down. The boat had dropped and Julio was stood by the controls screaming like a wild thing. He must have set the hydraulics off... somehow...I don't understand... he didn't know... Please don't blame him, I beg you! It's all my fault, not his. Mine!'

Broderick looked at the ruined man and spoke as clearly as he could. 'Yes. It is.'

The marked police car drew up and Calbot showed a WPC into the building as Broderick and Sullivan stood by the old Mercedes.

'Sir? I'm sorry, but can I be blunt?' Sullivan asked.

Broderick looked at her, but said nothing.

She continued. 'I'm sorry that nobody bothered to tell you I was arriving, sir. It's obvious that it's irritated you and I understand that. But I'd like you to know that this job is very important to me. It's not quite the brief I'd been expecting, but I'm glad about that. I'm not really one for just standing around and observing.'

Broderick raised an eyebrow. Sullivan continued.

'As I'm sure you've already realised. I just want you to know that I'm a professional police officer and I intend to work with you and assist you to the very best of my ability.'

Broderick simply stared at Sullivan. After a moment he scribbled a note, handed it to her and got into his car. It took only seconds for Sullivan to read the message. As she looked up to reply, Broderick closed his car door, turned the ignition and drove off. Calbot appeared at his colleague's shoulder.

'Another one? What's it say?' Calbot asked.

Sullivan handed her junior the note and walked off towards their parked car. Calbot looked down at the one line written on cheap notepaper and smiled at Broderick's untidy scrawl... *Keep your wig on, sergeant!*

Chapter 8

MARTIN TAVARES SAT staring at the television. The doctor had left him some tablets which he hadn't wanted to take. David had insisted, though. He needed to rest, to somehow switch off. He barely registered the local TV news going on, yet again, about his wife's death. His heart and mind felt overloaded with thoughts and feelings, none of which he could fully grasp.

'It would appear that this has been a tragic accident.' The voice of Chief Superintendent Massetti flowed from the box in the corner of the room. Martin observed the clear, crisp and professionally compassionate delivery of the police officer as she addressed the camera from the front of the Police Headquarters building. He thought she sounded like Margaret Thatcher, albeit with a slight Gibraltarian lilt.

'In attempting to avoid a collision, the police patrol bike hit Mrs Tavares, resulting in her death. At this stage I am entirely satisfied that the officers involved were not riding irresponsibly, but attempting to pursue the getaway motorcycle in very difficult circumstances.'

'Lying bitch,' David murmured under his breath, as he watched from the doorway.

'We believe the thieves may be part of an Eastern European criminal gang based on the Costa del Sol that targets luxury yachts and marinas. Their abandoned motorcycle was found earlier today and we are currently working with Spanish police to identify and apprehend the men in question. Once again, I wish to send our sincere condolences to Mr Tavares and his family at this very difficult time.'

Her interview over, Massetti moved swiftly back through the front gates of Police H.Q. Simultaneously, Broderick parked up his Mercedes in front of the building, narrowly missing contact with two of the television camera crew in the process.

Moments later, he marched across the central quad of the H.Q. and burst into the building. He was relieved to find Sergeant Aldarino not at his desk. Had he been there it would have meant at least half an hour with Massetti. Broderick had nothing against his commanding officer, but he hadn't got time to be a sounding board for her problems this morning. Not that she would have listened to much of the advise he might have given her. Massetti always dealt with him as though she was Dr Dolittle and he was a grumpy baboon. It was not a pleasant sensation.

Moving swiftly upstairs, he soon found the sanctuary of his office. Broderick was pleased to get back to it this morning as he could now get his hands on the 'prescription only' painkillers he kept secreted in his drawer. The wave of relief this brought him meant that he was willing to forgive the irritatingly bright and cheery dispositions of Calbot and Sullivan. Both officers beamed at him from their desks. Were they competing against one another for some kind of cuteness award?

'Morning, sir,' Sullivan announced airily.

'And a very good morning from me too, sir.' Calbot announced.

Broderick half sneered. There was a limit to how much he could take of this after all.

'What are you two looking so pleased about?'

'Just sorting the paper work on the Bassano case, sir,' Sullivan replied.

'And I'm getting the file on the Webster trial in order,' Calbot added. 'You're in court later in the week, guv.'

'Bugger.'

'Feeling better?' Sullivan asked.

'No, but at least the injections worn off so I won't be sounding like a half pissed Kermit all day.' He turned to Calbot. 'Get us a tea and a bacon sarnie, son.'

'I'm afraid sarnies are off the menu in the new canteen, guv. They do a very nice chorizo and avocado panini.'

Broderick simply stared at his DC.

'They also do a nice gluten free tuna salad wrap.'

A large file of papers flew across the room and struck Calbot on the side of his head.

'Ouch!' he whimpered.

'Ouch, my backside,' responded Broderick. 'Now get down there to Poncey Snacks Ltd and get me a sarnie and a mug of industrial strength cha.'

'Guv.'

Calbot backed meekly out of the office, knowing that he now had to run a quarter of a mile to the nearest greasy spoon cafe along by the docks. Broderick smiled to himself, fully aware of the mission that lay before his detective constable. And god forbid he should return with any part of the order cold. *Life's a bitch*, he thought, *and this morning I'm giving it a helping hand*. He turned to his slightly shocked detective sergeant.

'Read your file, er...?'

'*Sullivan*, sir.'

'I know your name,' Broderick insisted, reaching for Sullivan's papers. 'Impressive. One of the youngest women to join the Met CID. High flyer. Very ambitious.'

'Sir.'

'Then you nearly wreck it all by thinking you can do the job all by yourself.'

'It was a miscalculation, sir. I've learnt from it.'

'Chief Superintendent Reid writes about you in far from glowing terms, Sullivan. I quote: *By confronting the gunman alone, without back-up or respect to chain of command, DS Sullivan endangered not only her own life, but also that of the hostages and her fellow officers in the field of operations.*'

'I paid for that mistake, sir,' she responded bitterly.

'Passed over for promotion and a soft temporary posting over here? I'd say you've been lucky. Officers who don't pass the ball around really tend to — how can I put this? — piss me off. Is that clear enough for you?'

'Crystal, sir.'

'Good. Then we should rub along famously, shouldn't we?'

Sullivan returned her focus to her computer screen, wishing Broderick hadn't made his last remark sound like the challenge it clearly was. A moment later her thoughts were elsewhere.

Five Months Earlier

THE FIERCE RAIN was not helping things. It blurred the surroundings, making it hard to see more than a few metres ahead. Had it been daylight, things would have been easier. But here on an inlet of the River Roach, a fierce wind was blowing in off the North Sea and across the bleak and treacherous Essex coastline. The nearest hamlet was a few hundred yards back from the high banks of the river, too far to offer any glow of ambient light. The first officers on the scene had to navigate their way along the pitch black lane with hand torches. They soon found the car they had been searching for. The silver XJ Jaguar had nearly made it to the river's edge. The thick mud under its tyres had finally stopped it in its tracks, forcing the occupants to continue onwards on foot. The officers had information as to where they would be heading - information which was confirmed thirty metres on at the first sight of the Thames sailing barge, 'The Ness', moored to the river bank, its lights blazing from within.

By the time Sullivan arrived at the scene from London, the area had been cordoned off. Essex police had immediately requested armed marksmen to the riverside. They had duly arrived minutes earlier and were taking up strategic positions around the barge. Sullivan had been woken two hours earlier with the news that Malcolm Bainbridge, a multi-millionaire property developer, had gone on a shooting spree earlier in the evening. He had shot, at point blank range, two of his employees at Bainbridge Developments PLC. Returning home to his large Wimbledon mansion, he had shot a neighbour, a visiting friend and his housekeeper. Bainbridge had then attempted to burn his home down, before escaping into the night with his twelve year old daughter, Naomi, in the back seat of his car.

And now Bainbridge sat calmly aboard his beloved Thames barge with his shotgun on his lap and his traumatised daughter huddled in the corner. The last few hours had been a blur. A blinding rage. An overpowering madness that had only now begun to dissipate and be replaced by a cold understanding of what he had done. He also knew what he now had to do.

It had come as some surprise to Sullivan that Bainbridge had demanded to speak to her and her alone. She had met the man eight months earlier under tragic circumstances. The property tycoon's wife had been murdered in a car mugging that had gone terribly wrong. Stopping late at night at traffic lights, Madeleine Bainbridge had been attacked by two youths who had smashed the driver's window and pulled her from the car. Finding her cash card in her handbag, the thieves had demanded that she take them to a cashpoint and draw out money. Madeleine had stubbornly refused and been smashed over the head with a metal crowbar. She had died instantly. Sullivan had been an investigating officer on the case and had interviewed Bainbridge on several occasions. It was also a lead she had followed that eventually led to the arrest of the assailants.

And now she stood a few yards away from the barge, the chill November wind in her face, wondering what she could possibly do to end the terrible events of the night. Sullivan was quickly briefed by Chief Superintendent Reid on the things she couldn't do.

'Bainbridge has demanded that you speak to him,' Reid told her. 'In short, he has agreed to let his daughter go free if you replace her on board the barge.'

'I see,' Sullivan replied.

'That, of course, cannot happen. The risk to you would naturally be far greater than the potential threat to his own daughter.'

'Can you be sure of that?' Sullivan questioned. 'Has Bainbridge given any assurances?'

'He's told us that no harm would come to you. He says he needs to talk to someone who understands him. For some reason he considers that to be you.'

'With respect, sir, the main task here is to get that girl off the boat and out of harm's way. I'm prepared to co-operate with the exchange. I know him. I think I could persuade him to give himself up.'

'The man has just committed five murders. It's a classic psychotic killing rampage and I'm not prepared to let anyone else put themselves in danger's way. We'll stick to protocol and negotiate from here. You speak to him by phone. Understood?'

'I still feel...'

Reid interrupted her. 'That's an order, detective sergeant.'

For the next hour and a half Sullivan and the special police negotiator, DI Graham, had attempted to persuade the gunman to come ashore and give himself up. Bainbridge, however, was becoming increasingly irrational at the refusal to accept his demand.

'I need to speak to you alone, Sullivan,' Bainbridge's voice crackled through the mobile phone. 'I'm not kidding here. If you don't come aboard I'll have no choice but to kill Naomi and myself. You know I will. You've left me no where else to go.'

Something in his voice suggested to Sullivan that the end of the road was most definitely approaching. The man had sounded exhausted, and over the last few minutes had been increasingly distracted and rambling. Though no one mentioned it, she and her colleagues knew that Bainbridge would most likely follow through on his threat and that two more deaths were now imminent. Chief Superintendent Reid pulled Sullivan to one side.

'He's given us no real choice but to board the boat. Commander Laine has told me his men are in position and will make their assault on my order. You've done your best, Sullivan, but there's nothing more you can do.'

As Reid strode off towards the Commander, Sullivan realised what had to be done. An assault could lead to a bloodbath. She couldn't allow that to happen. Without further thought, Sullivan moved towards the barge. She held her hands high in the air. She was at the side of the boat before any of her fellow officers could attempt to stop her.

'Malcolm!' she called. 'It's me, Sullivan. I'm coming aboard.'

Behind her, she could hear Reid and DI Graham shouting for her to return to safety, but she would not obey.

'Let me on board and then release your daughter, Malcolm,' Sullivan called. 'I'm going to trust you to do that. Okay?"

From the boat Bainbridge yelled, 'How do I know you're not armed?'

'That's where you are going to have to trust me, Malcolm,' Sullivan replied.

Slowly, Sullivan walked the narrow plank connecting the river bank to the barge. Placing her hands once more above her head, she moved towards the lighted cabin. As she got to the doors, they were pushed open forcefully by Bainbridge, and Sullivan descended into the boat.

Inside, Bainbridge simply stared at her, his eyes on fire. After a few desperate moments of silence he murmured, 'Thank you.'

Naomi was still huddled in a corner of the cabin. Sullivan looked across to the petrified girl.

'Let her go, Malcolm. She's your daughter. It's what Madeleine would want, you know that.'

The mention of his wife's name seemed to calm the man. It seemed as though by using it, Sullivan had confirmed that his wife was somehow still with him. Two minutes later, Naomi Bainbridge made her way ashore to be greeted by police officers and a paramedic. Back on the barge, Sullivan and Naomi's father sat and talked. They talked for two more hours, Sullivan listening to the man's story of madness brought on by grief and despair. The anger and rage that had filled his life since the murder of his dear wife. He talked of the blackouts and missing periods that had begun to haunt him during the last few months. He talked of death as being his only choice.

At four seventeen a.m. precisely, Detective Sergeant Sullivan escorted Malcolm Bainbridge ashore to be met by an armed police escort. No further life would be lost that night. Her fellow officers congratulated her on her immense bravery - all except Chief Superintendent Reid. Grave-faced, the commanding officer pulled her to one side.

'You may think that you're a hero, Sullivan. Don't fool yourself. What you did tonight was unprofessional and foolhardy in the extreme. You disobeyed a direct order from me and seriously put at risk the entire operation.'

'Please, sir...'

'Don't interrupt me, officer!' Reid shouted, red-faced. 'Just because you managed to pull it off doesn't mean it was the right thing to do. You risked the lives of everyone here on a simple hunch. If it had gone wrong, who knows what catastrophic events may have occurred? I'm going to make sure that this is investigated, Sullivan and, when it is, your career as a police officer will be finished. You may think that the end justifies the means, but that's not how this police force operates and never will. Now get out of my sight.'

Sullivan moved to the waiting police car. She knew Reid was right. She knew she had been a fool. But right now, as she looked across at Naomi Bainbridge being treated for shock in the back of the waiting ambulance, she couldn't give a damn.

Sullivan was at her desk, her back turned towards Broderick. The sun shining through the office window was warm on her face as she went through the motions of organising her desk. In reality, she was letting her mind wander back to that night on the River Roach five months before. It was a process she had repeated a hundred times. She had asked every question as to how differently she might have handled the situation. In the cold light of day, it was clear that she had thrown the rule book into the river and then jumped in herself. At the time, the danger of the situation and the adrenalin running through her system had made her feel certain of her actions. It was madness and she'd known it, but her instincts had pulled her firmly away from the procedures she would normally have unquestioningly followed to the letter. Her intervention had undeniably brought the situation to a positive close — for the twelve year old hostage at least — and most probably kept her fellow officers from having to step into the firing line. The accusations made by her superiors, that lives had been put at risk, had hurt the most.

Breaking the rules, she would plead guilty to. Risking her colleagues' lives was something she knew she would never have countenanced. Therefore it was a great relief when the official enquiry into the events had cleared her of that last charge. The fact that it found her guilty of breaking the chain of command and wilful insubordination was something she could not deny and would have to live with.

So here she was, a thousand miles south of London, sharing a cramped office with two strangers. Cast aside in a distant country, far from her home and the old sureties that life was unfolding exactly as it should. Back in the Met she would have made inspector by now. Here in Gibraltar, she was reduced to helping out an old school operator like Broderick and a pushy upstart like Calbot. At least the climate might enable her to get a little tan on her legs, she thought. That and the chance to regroup and plan for some kind of future. She might even follow in her predecessor's footsteps and find an alternative form of employment down here on the shores of the Mediterranean.

Sullivan's reverie was broken by the sudden entrance of Calbot. He was carrying a polystyrene cup and a strange smelling, roughly wrapped sandwich.

'One tea – two sugars – and a *jamon* sarnie for the guv'nor!' he announced.

Sullivan smiled. *Just go with the flow*, she thought. *Go with the flow.*

The slight thud and click of the heavy front door preceded by seconds the large hallway clock chiming the hour. It was seven a.m. precisely. The old lady stood on the upstairs landing. She had been waiting there, hardly daring to breath for fear of drawing attention to herself. But now the house was hers once more and she relaxed for the first time in hours.

She had been awake most of the night, as usual, though the screams from the far bedroom had been far less intrusive than of late. The demon had left the house and would not return for at least ten hours. Sometimes, if she was lucky, it would not return for days. But return it would, bringing danger and malice as its gifts.

The old lady was uncharacteristically hungry, but breakfast would have to wait. She did not want to have to manage the stairs too many times in a day. Besides, her chores for now were centred upstairs. As she moved slowly down the corridor towards the door, the sense of dread at what she might find behind it gripped her as it always did. She would tidy and clean, mend and sew if needed. But these were simple physical tasks, achieved with ease. The blackness and pain that hung heavily in the room at the end of the corridor were metaphysical. Stains which could not be tidied away or expunged nearly so easily.

It had been a week since Sullivan had first set foot on the Rock. A week spent mostly improving the efficiency of Chief Inspector Broderick's office. After the quick conclusion of the boathouse death, things had been a little slow. Too slow for Sullivan's liking. If this was the pace of police life on Gibraltar, her secondment was going to be boring in the extreme.

Today she was moving from the hotel to a small fourth floor apartment overlooking the old naval dockyards a few hundred metres from Police HQ . She had loved the apartment on sight. It even had a balcony and a small plunge pool in the ground floor courtyard. Quite a contrast from her London studio flat back in Wood Green.

Broderick had given her the morning off to effect the move, and she had used it to work out in the hotel gym and do some shopping for the apartment. Having settled her extras bill, she was now sitting in the hotel reception waiting for a taxi to take her to the South District. Glancing at the front page of the daily newspaper, she noticed that the funeral of the local woman who had been killed by a police motorcycle was to take place that morning. She had, of course, been told all about it at HQ. She had even been introduced to one of the officers involved one lunchtime in the canteen. She had felt sorry for him. He'd had a haunted look about him and seemed totally wiped out by the incident. Both officers had subsequently been suspended pending the results of a police investigation.

The doorman approached Sullivan and announced that her taxi had arrived. Picking up her cases, he led her out of the Hotel Alameda to the waiting car. Once there, he loaded the bags and happily received a generous tip. Tamara Sullivan was in an unusually good mood.

The atmosphere outside the crematorium was fittingly sombre as Bryant and Ferra observed the relatives and friends of the Tavares family arriving for the ceremony. The two police officers stood a discreet distance away from the building. They had come to pay their respects, but didn't want to draw attention to themselves. Though they knew they would not be welcome, it was something they had felt needed to be done. Looking across towards the crematorium, Ferra was now having doubts.

'Look, Bryant, I can't do this, okay?'

'Well, I've got to,' Bryant replied.

'I'm sorry. I thought I could, but I just can't.'

Bryant nodded his reluctant understanding as Ferra headed back down the street to his car. Bryant braced himself to face the music on his own.

As the last of the mourners entered the building, he crossed the street and entered the building. There was standing room only as the service begun and Bryant joined those mourners at the back of the crematorium. Hoping that he might leave unnoticed before the end, Bryant breathed a little easier. As the minutes went by, it soon became clear that his plan would not work.

Word of the police officer's presence quickly spread around the crematorium. A slow whisper travelled around the chapel, finally reaching the front row. Sitting next to the grieving Martin Tavares, David turned to see the policeman and then whispered the news to his brother-in-law. Immediately Tavares spun round and launched himself up the aisle towards Bryant - his face flushed with fury.

'Get out! You're not welcome here! Can't you leave us in peace, for God's sake?'

Murmurs and shocked whispers reverberated around the chapel as David caught up with Martin and restrained him. Making a sharp exit, Bryant glanced back to see Martin Tavares's eyes boring into his.

'You're a murderer! I hope you die, you bastard!'

The bright lights illuminating the signs on the outside of Gino's Bar began to flicker off as Bryant stumbled out of his watering hole of choice. Gino had been trying to close up for an hour and a half. It was nearly three thirty in the morning and the bar owner had little sympathy for the state Bryant had got himself into.

The walk home took the suspended police officer twice as long as it usually did, his legs seemingly incapable of supporting him for more than a few paces as he zig-zagged and stumbled down the narrow passageways. The brandy was causing the blood to pound in his head, numbing his every thought and feeling. Just what he had wanted.

As he reached his apartment and took out his key, the drunken officer did not notice the curtain flickering at his living room window. Nor did he notice the figure watching him from the shadows of his hallway as he struggled through the apartment's front door.

Fumbling like a blind man, Bryant headed straight for the kitchen. Opening the fridge, he took out a carton of milk and poured it into a pan. His microwave had partially exploded a month before, so he was reduced to warming it the old-fashioned way — an electric hob on his cooker. Bryant needed a hot drink. It would settle him and help him sleep. Moving into the sitting room, he switched on the radio for company and then looked around him. The room seemed different somehow. He couldn't begin to work out exactly how it was different, but then he couldn't work anything out in the state he was in. It was all he could do to remain upright. He gave in at last and slumped into his all-enveloping armchair.

He had barely managed to kick off his shoes before he felt the rope tightening around his neck.

CHAPTER 9.

THE FLASH OF blue lights from the assembled police cars and ambulance bounced off the white plaster walls of the surrounding buildings, as Broderick's Mercedes pulled up outside the apartment. It was six a.m. and the chief inspector had been summoned from his bed. A clearly agitated Calbot was on the pavement, waiting for him.

'It's definitely Bryant, sir,' the detective constable informed him. 'The building's superintendent found him when she entered his apartment after the fire alarm went off. Said the place could have burnt down. Bryant had left a pan of milk on the stove.'

'Have the Glee Club arrived?' Broderick replied. 'Laytham's here and forensics are on their way. Not worth the journey, I'd have thought. Looks like suicide. Jesus, the poor bastard.'

'He was a friend of yours, wasn't he?' Broderick asked. Calbot nodded his head.

'Why don't you bugger off? Leave this to me and Sullivan.'

'Thanks, guv, but he was my mate. I feel I should...' Calbot could not finish. He was clearly moved.

'Understood,' Broderick sympathised. 'At least stay out here.'

Calbot pulled himself up.

'I'll do my job, guv. Thanks anyway.'

Broderick nodded, and both men entered the building. A moment later they were in Bryant's apartment and moving through into the living room. Music was playing from somewhere in the apartment. A melody Broderick recognised from decades back. Electric Light Orchestra? Supertramp? Something like that.

Entering the living room, the sight before him, although expected, still managed to shock. Bryant's lifeless body hung from the ceiling. His legs swung in limbo over a fallen chair as the breeze came in through an open window. The police photographer was at work recording the grisly image. Broderick noticed that the rope around Bryant's neck had been looped over a large hook in the ceiling, then fed back to the bedroom door where it had been tied off and secured around the handle. The hook had clearly been installed specially for the job and as such had proved fit for purpose. It suggested to Broderick that the dead officer had put some real thought into creating the macabre scene.

'Morning, Chief Inspector,' Professor Laytham boomed.

'Morning, Prof. Been in the wars?'

Laytham had a plaster on his forehead. Typical of the pathologist, the dressing had been attached at a rather jaunty angle.

'Slipped in the bloody shower this morning, such was the rush to get here. Could have achieved a most ignominious end for myself, Chief Inspector. Still, not as bad as this poor fellow. One of yours, I hear?'

Broderick looked across the room to where a radio was still playing in the corner.

'Will somebody turn that bloody thing off?'

Calbot swiftly obliged as his boss turned back to Laytham.

'Suicide?'

'I'd say. Typical of its kind. A painful one, too, I fear. They always think it's going to be quick, but they never give themselves a long enough drop. To break the neck, I mean. That's the hangman's skill. Too long, mind, and you'll snap the head clean off.' As Laytham said this, he snapped his fingers in an attempt to recreate the noise.

'Yes, well.' Broderick turned to his DC. 'Calbot? Did he leave a note? Anything at all?'

'Not that we've found, guv.'

'Right. Well, keep looking.'

Broderick looked troubled. Moving back into the hall, he entered the small kitchen. The burnt out pan had been placed in the sink. There was some damage to the electric hob, but nothing major. There had obviously been more smoke than fire. There was another door coming off the kitchen. Much to his surprise, Broderick found it wasn't locked. It opened onto a shared communal yard full of bins and detritus. A few yards down he could see a door in the wall which most probably led out onto a side street.

'He was a good bloke, you know, guv.' Calbot was at his boss's shoulder.

'Didn't know you mixed with uniformed.'

'Not if I can help it. We just liked the footie, that's all. He was a United supporter, like me.'

'Not really a good enough reason to commit suicide, Calbot.'

Calbot momentarily appreciated the black humour.

'Heh.'

Broderick checked the kitchen cupboards. All plates, pots and pans in regimental order. He was also aware of a distinct smell. A sort of disinfectant. He'd noticed it first in the living room, but it was stronger in the kitchen. An old-fashioned smell, at least to Broderick's senses, but an aroma that was familiar. He just couldn't place it. The Chief Inspector turned to Calbot.

'We all knew he'd taken the Tavares accident badly. Did he give any indication that it might lead to this?'

'Not to me, guv. He wasn't himself, but he seemed to be getting on with it.'

'You ever been here before?' Broderick asked. 'To this apartment?'

'Once or twice. To watch a game. Have a drink.'

'The place is immaculate. Even his DVD collection is in alphabetical order,' Broderick observed. 'Neat as a pin, was he?'

'I wouldn't say that, guv. Tell the truth, the place was always a bit of a pit. His locker at the station is much the same. We take the piss out of him about...'

Calbot stopped, realising the need to now use the past participle.

'...*took* the piss out of him about it. Shit. Sorry, guv, but why didn't he just talk to us? He didn't have to do this.' Broderick patted the younger man on the shoulder. 'You get back to the station. Clear your head.'

'No thanks, sir. I'd rather keep busy if it's alright with you?'

'Okay. Check and see if Bryant used a cleaner. Someone he hired to tidy the pit.'

'Will do.'

Calbot moved off as Broderick re-entered the living room. Looking once more at the scene, Broderick mused to himself.

'Or maybe the accident changed Bryant in more ways than one.'

Sullivan appeared behind him at the door. She did her best to avoid looking directly at the hanging corpse.

'Been talking to the apartment superintendent, sir. She lives directly opposite. Says that she was woken by Bryant coming home. He made quite a lot of noise getting into the building, apparently. She thought he'd been drinking.'

'What time was this?'

'She says it was just after four. Ten minutes or so later the fire alarm went off, so she got her pass key and gained entry.'

'Milk on the stove.'

'Yes, sir.'

Broderick gathered his thoughts.

'So that means Bryant arrived back home, put some milk on the stove to warm it, switched his radio on and then decided to top himself?'

'Looks that way, sir,' Sullivan replied.

Broderick turned to see Bryant's body being carefully lifted down from the hook in the ceiling.

'Yeah...I suppose it does.'

Massetti sat at her desk, her headache beginning to take on migraine proportions.

'So what are you saying, Broderick?'

'I'm just voicing my concerns, ma'am.'

Broderick had seen Massetti under pressure many times before, but never quite to this extent. He knew he had to tread carefully. Massetti looked up at her Chief Inspector.

'If you're saying what I think you're saying — that Bryant's death was the result of something else — then you'd better have more than just a feeling of unease about it. What's Laytham come up with?'

'Bit early doors, but he's pretty certain it's death caused by hanging. Suicide, in his view.'

'In his view, but not in yours?'

'Not yet, ma'am.'

Massetti stood, and moved to her office window. 'And the forensics boys?'

'Nothing of significance from the Glee Club yet, ma'am.'

'Please don't refer to them as that, Broderick.'

'Nothing significant from forensics,' Broderick corrected. 'No prints other than Bryants. We're still waiting on the rest.'

'Doesn't look wonderfully promising, does it?'

'No, but I'd like to keep this open for a bit longer. See if we can get something from it,' Broderick replied.

'I don't need to tell you that it's a little inconvenient, Chief Inspector. Especially considering the press interest in the case.' Broderick stayed silent. Massetti sighed. 'All right. But I can't wait forever, you understand?'

'Ma'am.'

Gibraltar. 1966.

THE SUN SHINES through the open French windows, warming the boy's face. He's barely ten years old, and his father is sat beside him, his arm round his son's shoulder. The boy tries to release his tears, but tears will not come.

In the centre of the room a police inspector leans over the woman's body. The boy cannot bear to look. A trickle of blood falls down her cheek, a final crimson animation from her lifeless corpse.

The boy clings helplessly to his father as a uniformed police officer leads the man from the room towards the hallway. Another policeman takes the boy and carries him kicking and screaming out onto the terrace. The hot air hits the boy's face, but inside — deep inside — he feels chilled to the core.

He had seen his father's eyes. The relief. The calm. His father who had reached for his son, protecting him as he always did. That protection was gone now. The boy was on his own. Alone.

CHAPTER 10

ALTHOUGH IT WAS only early evening, the Marina Bar was busier than Calbot and Sullivan had expected — its customers mostly German or Swedish cruise ship tourists, lingering on dry land for a cocktail or two before heading back to their floating hotels.

'One white wine spritzer,' Calbot announced as he returned to the table with the drinks.

'Thanks,' Sullivan replied, raising a small smile.

Calbot lifted a pint of ice cold lager to his lips.   'Cheers.'

Sullivan's eyes narrowed.

'So, DC Calbot, what's all this in aid of?'

Calbot drew a breath. 'Well, it occurred to me that you hadn't really been welcomed to the Rock, Sarge. In the traditional way.'

'With a good old-fashioned police piss-up, you mean?'

Calbot shrugged his shoulders.

'Well, thanks for the thought. There is, of course, one notable absentee,.

'The guv? Oh, no, no. He doesn't do social. Too busy at home.'

'Family?'

'Sort of. Lives with his sister.'

'Oh yeah?' Sullivan questioned, trying not to sound too intrigued.

'Before he joined the RGP he was in the Met for eighteen years. Then his wife walked out on both him and their two daughters. His mum was born on the Rock and his sister's lived in Gib since the nineties, so basically, he moved over here so that his sis could help him with the girls. Particularly the youngest one. Down's Syndrome.'

'Oh,' Sullivan replied. Whatever she might have been expecting to hear about her boss's private life, this scenario was not on the list. 'And his wife?'

'Vanished. Apparently he spent years trying to find her. But as you'll know, if a person wants to disappear completely it's not that hard to achieve these days. He never talks about it. They've lived with the sister up in the Old Town for eight years now.'

'I see.'

A group of tourists at the next table erupted with loud laughter. Calbot took the cue to lighten things up.

'And as for me — since I'm sure you'll be fascinated to know - I'm half Gibraltarian too. Grew up in the UK, but my dad insisted we spent every summer holiday here on the Rock. When I decided to join the police, it was a no brainer. The mean streets of London or the sunny streets of Gib.'

Sullivan smiled. The wine was working fast. She was feeling relaxed for the first time in as long as she could remember.

'What about you?' Calbot continued. 'Complicated, I heard?'

Sullivan raised an eyebrow.

'You have no idea. So...' she said, raising her glass. 'Here's to changing the subject.'

Broderick parked his Mercedes in the narrow driveway of his sister's three storey Victorian town house. Glancing in the rear view mirror, he was surprised to see how tired he looked. A good old fashioned haircut was also on the cards. His head of once thick brown hair now resembled the metallic mesh of a saucepan scourer. As he pulled himself out of the car, a motorbike screeched to a halt in the driveway behind him. Before Broderick had a chance to fully register this information, the front door of the house was flung open and his eighteen-year-old daughter, Penny, rushed to greet the motorcyclist - her boyfriend, Raoul.   'Laters, Dad!'

'Wait a sec, Penny. Where are you off to?'

'Raoul's got tickets for the Killers,' she answered excitedly as she clambered onto the back of the bike.

'The what?'

'The Killers, Dad. They're a band!'

'Really? Look just take care of her on that thing, Raoul, will you?'

Penny threw her dad the look she reserved for when she thought he was fussing too much. It was a look Broderick had become very well acquainted with. Before he could riposte, she was on the back of the bike.

'Yeah, yeah, Dad! Bye!'

With a rev of the motorcycle engine, they were gone. Shaking his head, Broderick made his way through the front door, down the long hallway and into the kitchen, where his sister was sitting preparing an evening meal. Although ten years older than her brother, Cath looked the younger of the siblings. Having married a Gibraltarian lawyer, she had lived on the Rock for nearly a quarter of a century, Widowed far too young, she had welcomed the role of aunty and homemaker to her nieces and brother. Being half Gibraltarian, both sister and brother had also felt the benefit of having family nearby.

'Hello, love.' Cath smiled. 'Good day at work?'

'Not great. You?'

'You look tired,' Cath replied, ignoring the question.

'Makes a change, does it?'

'You work too hard, you know you do. I take it you bumped into her Royal Highness? Out for a night with Justin Bieber.'

Broderick had little idea who she was talking about and even less inclination to enquire. 'Where's Daisy?'

'Upstairs in her bedroom, putting her glad rags on,' Cath replied, placing a basket of bread and a small saucer of olive oil on the table.

'For what?'

'She says she's going clubbing.'

'Clubbing?'

'She's been waiting for you to get in.' Cath raised an eyebrow by way of wishing her brother good luck in the matter.

Broderick nodded, turned on his heels and headed into the hallway and up the stairs. As he reached his younger daughter's bedroom, he tapped lightly on the door and entered.

Fourteen-year-old Daisy was sat on her bed, wearing a bright yellow and blue party dress, her hair shining and specially combed.

'Daddy!' cried Daisy, as she jumped up to hug her father.

'Hello, sunshine. Looking good!'

And she was. From the moment Daisy was born she had been his little angel. The pain and worry that he and her mother had felt during pregnancy had disappeared for Broderick the moment she had been born. He knew instinctively that this little girl, with her extra chromosome, would be special.

And here she was, fourteen already, bright, loving, demanding, intelligent and like her sister Penny, the apple of his eye. The same had sadly not been true for Daisy's mother. Black depression and self-hatred had followed the birth. Unable to accept that her Down's Syndrome daughter was anything other than a punishment for some sin she felt she must have committed, she had struggled for nearly two years to come to terms with life. Unable to cope, she had one day disappeared from their lives, leaving two children without a mother and Broderick without the love of his life.

'Going dancing, Daddy!' Daisy announced, a smile beaming across her face as she sat back on the bed.

'Oh, good. Where?'

'Disco. Going to get a boyfriend.'

'Ah. I thought you had a boyfriend at school? Nicky, isn't it?'

'Nah. He's not a good one. I want a disco boyfriend. I'm going to love him.'

Broderick sat on the bed next to his daughter and put his arm round her. 'Well, that's good. That's good. But it is a Friday night, you know.'

'Yeah. I know.'

'I could put a DVD on in a minute if you like. Harry Potter, maybe?'

Her face lit up. 'Yeah, Harry!'

'I thought I'd get some fish and chips from Roy's as well.'

'Fish and chips.'

'And a bottle of cream soda,' Broderick added, relishing his daughter's delight.

'Yeah!'

'Fancy that, Daisy?'

'Yeah! Fish and riding whips!'

'Yeah,' Broderick smiled, kissing Daisy on her forehead. 'Fish and riding whips.'

Sullivan and Calbot were still tucked away in a corner table of the Marina Bar. They had spent over an hour in each other's company. There was nothing unusual in this. They worked together side by side on a daily basis. What was unusual was that it was out of 'office hours' and to her great surprise Sullivan had found herself enjoying her colleague's company. Calbot's infuriating cockiness had given way to a natural charm and ease that was usually absent in his dealings with her. So it came as something of a surprise to discover that the time was later than she had expected. After she turned down Calbot's offer of another drink, they both stood and moved to the door, passing a fellow officer at the far end of the bar. PC Ferra was nursing a large brandy and seemed to be lost in his thoughts. Calbot broke his colleague's reverie as he placed a hand on the officer's shoulder.

'Ferra? I'm sorry about Bryant.'

'So am I. He was a good man.'

'If you need anything...?'

Ferra nodded, as Calbot and Sullivan forced a smile and moved towards the door and out onto the street.

'Thanks for the initiation ceremony,' Sullivan said as they got outside.

'You're very welcome. Share a taxi home?' Calbot offered.

'Nah, I'll walk. And so should you.'

Calbot gave her a quizzical look.

'Clear your head,' Sullivan added.

'Yeah. You know, it's funny. Thought you'd be Irish, name like Sullivan.'

'My dad was born in Dublin.'

'Nice.'

'My mum's from Nassau. In the Bahamas.'

'Exotic.'

'I was brought up in London and on the Wirral.'

'Wherever you're from, you're not what I thought you'd be.'

'Meaning what, exactly?' Sullivan challenged half-heartedly.

'Nothing....nothing really.' Calbot attempted a change of topic. 'I enjoyed that. You should be initiated more often.'

The awkward pause that followed was broken by Sullivan.

'Right. Well. Good night, Detective Constable.'

'Night, then.'

Calbot crossed the street towards the sports bars on the other side The night was obviously still young for him. Sullivan waited a moment. Had Calbot really given her the come on? Had she perhaps encouraged it? Had she not learnt by now how dangerous the after work drinks with fellow officers could prove? She shuddered a little inside and headed off in the other direction for home.

Ferra knew he shouldn't drive — not after the amount he'd drunk, so it came as a relief to bump into some friends leaving the bar next door. They promptly offered him a lift. Ferra's home, a boat - wasn't far, but he needed sleep now and quickly. His mooring was half a mile away on the Kingsway Wharf. The 'Ailsa', a 1960's built four-berther, had been his home for three years now. It belonged to his great uncle, who had a long lease on the mooring at a ridiculously low — by Gib standards — annual rent. Ferra paid next to nothing for his lodgings in return for keeping the old man's boat seaworthy.

Ferra's pals dropped him off and as their car drove away, the policeman walked carefully down the third avenue of pontoon moorings. It wasn't late, but the place was deserted. The nearby boats were mostly owned by local Gibraltarians who would turn out during the day, but be off home come the dark. There were other fellow boat residents in the basin, but they had either turned in already or were elsewhere. Taking a deep breath, and being careful not to slip, Ferra stepped aboard the 'Ailsa' and tried to find his keys, with no success. Distracted by the sudden sound of an object hitting the deck of the boat, he turned to see what it might be. As he did so, he felt a sudden blow to the back of his legs. Falling to his knees, he was stunned to feel a rope being slipped over his head. Managing to stagger upwards he flailed out at his assailant, but before any contact could be made his head was violently yanked upwards as the rope was tightened around his neck.

Turning and twisting in desperation, Ferra felt his feet lift from the ground as a forceful push propelled him over the side of the boat and into mid-air. The rope jolted sharply as the policeman's neck snapped in an instant.

CHAPTER 11

THE HOT WATER cascaded down Sullivan's back as she threw her head back and exhaled. Her morning shower was a sheer pleasure and she wasn't going to miss a second of it. She had been up at five thirty and half-way through her daily three mile jog by six. She varied her jogging route once or twice a week and as such had got to know Gibraltar quite well. It was, in fact, even smaller than she had imagined. The combination of its densely packed population and housing, together with the presence of international financial services, the shipping trade, tourism and the large naval docks and military garrison, gave Gibraltar a diversity and energy that would not have been out of place in a major city. It wasn't just the sunshine that had made Sullivan feel at ease upon the Rock. Increasingly it was both the place and its people.

But now, as she rinsed the shampoo from her long dark hair, she caught a glimpse of her showered body in the bathroom mirror. Tall, muscular and athletic was the shape that met her eye. A far cry from the modish anorexic look so favoured by the high fashion houses and movie world. Besides, she rarely looked at herself these days, vanity being an indulgence she had long given up on. She knew she was attractive, that much was clear by the way many men and some women treated her on first meeting. She also knew better than most that good looks in her trade could prove more of a handicap than a virtue. She had often thought that had she possessed a face like a pug dog and a body like a shot putter, she would have made it to Inspector by now. Not that her own actions hadn't slowed the speed of her career advancement to a near standstill by themselves. For now, she felt good and looked okay, so why dwell on the negative? The water was hot, breakfast was waiting, and order had been restored to her life.

Seconds later her mobile phone started to ring in the next room, the insistent noise immediately grating on her nerves. She reached for a towel, wrapped it around her and rushed to answer it, her wet footprints leaving marks on the tiled floor. She reached for the phone.

'Sullivan.'

Calbot was on the line. There had been an incident. Sullivan had dropped her towel and was moving swiftly to her bedroom before Calbot had even finished with the details.

Sullivan pushed her way through the crowds of onlookers milling along the wharf, as she headed for the flashing lights of the ambulance and police cars. It was Broderick who spoke first when she got to the boat.

'Can't we get the poor bastard down from there?'

For the second time since her arrival on the colony, Sullivan saw the wretchedly distressing sight of a hanging corpse. Ferra's eyes bulged from their sockets and his tongue lolled from his mouth. His dead body hung limply from the mast and boom, and had obviously been pushed out and over the side so that his feet dangled helplessly just a few feet above the water.

'Laytham's been delayed, sir. With respect, I think we should wait,' a uniformed officer replied.

Broderick nodded and turned to see the growing crowd of onlookers beginning to edge down the pontoon towards the horrific scene.

'Well, at least let's clear the bloody audience away,' Broderick barked. 'Calbot, sort them out, will you?'

'Yes, sir,' Calbot replied, obediently.

Sullivan joined her superior, and the pair stepped on board the boat.

'I don't believe it, sir. Me and Calbot only saw him last night.'

'Yes, Calbot told me. Do you know if Massetti has been informed?'

'No idea, sir.'

'Yeah, well our beloved Chief Super is going to love this,' Broderick said, tailing off as he examined the rope from which Ferra's grey, lifeless body was swaying. 'Doesn't look like boating line. If you ask me, it's pretty much identical to the one used on Bryant.'

'Or the one that Bryant used, sir?'

'As my sixteen year old daughter would say, Sullivan... *Whatever!* But let's check it out, eh? Or is that beyond your brief?'

Before Sullivan had a chance to answer, Calbot's voice called out from the end of the pontoon. 'Sir? I think you should have a look at this.'

'Christ's sake, what now?' Broderick snarled as he carefully left the boat and walked over to where Calbot was standing beside a severed wire running along the side of the wooden pontoon.

'It's the wire connecting the communal lights in the marina. It's been cut.'

Broderick knelt to examine it.

'Looks like someone's just sliced through.'

'Guy on the boat over there says the lights had been fine when he turned in at ten last night.' Calbot nodded to an elderly gentleman who was speaking to a uniformed officer taking notes. From behind him, they noticed Professor Laytham jogging up the marina towards them. Broderick observed that the older man was clearly a lot fitter than he was. And he smoked a pipe. Was there no bloody justice?

'Sorry for the delay. Went to the wrong marina... mooring... thingy,' Laytham offered as he looked over towards Ferra's body. 'Oh dear, oh dear.'

'Looks like this one managed the requisite drop, eh, Professor?' Broderick observed.

'Oh, absolutely. Much cleaner job this time. Quite impressive, poor sod.'

'Do you think you could get on with it? We'd like to get him down as soon as possible,' Broderick ordered. He was now tetchy both with the situation and the sudden flaring up of his irritable bowel syndrome.

'Oh yes, by all means,' Laytham replied. 'You look a little pale yourself, if you don't mind my saying so, Inspector.'

Broderick gave the pathologist a look that suggested further concern would not be appreciated.

'I'll get stuck in then,' mumbled Laytham, and moved swiftly towards the boat.

As Broderick and Sullivan watched Ferra's body being carried to the ambulance, a uniformed police constable approached them.

'Excuse me, sir?'

'Yes?' Broderick asked.

'I was out with Ferra last night, sir. Well not actually out with him, just gave him a lift back here from the Marina Bar. Can't believe it.'

'Yes. Well, I'm sorry.'

'I, uh... found these in my car this morning, sir. I think they're his,' the officer said, handing Broderick a set of keys.

'Thank you, constable.' When the officer had left, Broderick turned to Sullivan. 'Get Calbot to organise a door to door, will you?'

'Door to door, sir?'

'Well, boat to boat, whatever. See if anyone saw anything out of the ordinary last night. Oh, and hurry the Glee Club along, will you?'

'Are you treating this as a crime scene, sir?' Sullivan asked.

'Bloody well looks that way, doesn't it?'

Thirty minutes later, Broderick and Sullivan were still on the deck of the 'Ailsa'. One of the keys the young policeman had handed his Chief Inspector had matched the lock of the boat's cabin. Not that it had proved necessary, as the cabin door had already been open. Down below, Broderick had been struck by the immaculate nature of the boat's interior. This came as no surprise, as the limited confines of the living quarters dictated that to avoid chaos, order must be maintained. Broderick also noted that the late officer's CD and DVD collection was meticulous in its alphabetic correctness and - more interestingly — the same faint smell of disinfectant he had noticed at Bryant's apartment lingered in the shadowy interior of Ferra's boat as well.

Back on deck, Broderick felt a sharp pain in his abdomen and blinked in the sunlight. Sullivan noticed his discomfort.

'Are you alright, sir?' she questioned.

'A damn sight better than Ferra, so I'm not complaining.'

Broderick took a deep lungful of the fresh sea air and turned to his detective sergeant.

'So, what have we got so far? Ferra gets back from a night out, arrives here at his boat, climbs on board and hangs himself from the cross mast.'

'So it would seem,' Sullivan replied.

'We know he'd dropped his keys in the car on his way home, so how did he open the cabin? How likely is it that he'd leave his boat unlocked all day?'

'A spare key somewhere?' Sullivan offered.

'Anybody found one?'

'No, sir.'

Broderick looked out to sea, his mind trying to compose logic. 'So, like Bryant, he makes a noose from some rope and decides to end it all.'

'Well, yes, but...'

'And like Bryant, no note.'

'Suicide isn't always planned out in advance, sir. It's a fact that sometimes the act is a spontaneous action. And even if there is no note here at the scene, there could be one elsewhere. Also, it's far from unprecedented for friends to follow the tragic actions of another. Bryant killed himself and Ferra was drawn to the same fate, perhaps?'

'I'm not saying you're wrong, Sullivan. It's just that I have a saying. What you see is usually what you've got. Inside my head I have this small insistent voice telling me that in this case...it's not.'

CHAPTER 12

BRODERICK SIPPED A double espresso at a corner table of the police canteen as Sullivan reiterated her theories about the deaths of Ferra and Bryant.

'Both were traumatised by the accident and the death of Mrs Tavares, we know that much. Bryant took his life and Ferra decided to follow him. I saw him last night, guv, and he didn't look too great.'

'It's possible, but it just doesn't ring true somehow.'

'Or maybe... who knows... they made some sort of double suicide pact. Stranger things have happened.'

'Indeed they have.'

Calbot entered the busy canteen and strode towards his colleagues.

'Something interesting, guv.'

'Oh yeah?' Broderick didn't even look up.

'A woman across the marina saw a man walking away from Ferra's boat at about eleven thirty-five last night. Thought he looked a bit odd. It was too dark and too far away to get any useful description, apparently.'

'Have the CCTV checks come back yet?' Broderick asked.

'That's just the thing, guv. The CCTV in that part of the marina was down last night. Unidentifiable technical glitch, apparently.'

Broderick threw his hands up in despair.

'Great. Bloody great. One step forward, two steps back.'

'Oh...and Massetti is wanting to see you, guv,' Calbot added. 'Seemed quite agitated. In fact, I think it's the first time I've ever heard her swear.'

Calbot headed off. Broderick unhurriedly continued to drink his coffee.

Fifty minutes later, Broderick stopped Massetti as she crossed the central courtyard of police headquarters. His commanding officer knew exactly what the Chief Inspector had on his mind.

'These men died of asphyxia and a broken neck respectively, Broderick. Both injuries caused by hanging. Most likely cause, suicide. You heard it yourself from the pathologist.'

'There's no question that they were hung, ma'am. However, we have an unidentified man walking away from Ferra's boat just minutes after his arrival. Also, the rope used in both hangings appears to be of the same type. And in Ferra's case, it wasn't a type of rope usually considered appropriate for marine use.'

Massetti paused for a moment. 'And forensics?'

'Forensics are yet to report. Sullivan's chasing them up.'

'Right. Well, we'll wait for that, shall we?'

'The marina's pedestrian lighting had been cut off, ma'am. The CCTV was conveniently out of action and neither of the men left suicide notes.'

Massetti moved off towards the archway and front gates that led to the street. Broderick followed.

'So what you're saying is...'

'Maybe they weren't suicides, ma'am. Maybe they were both the victims of some kind of execution.'

Massetti turned to face Broderick, folding her arms across her chest. 'By whom, exactly?'

'Someone who's decided to set themselves up as judge and jury.'

'Martin Tavares, you mean?'

'Well, I certainly think we should question him, ma'am.'

'On what grounds exactly? You're playing with fire as usual, Broderick. You have no understanding of the pressure this force is under right now. And on this one, *I'm* where the buck stops. Do you understand? The irony is that the press are actually feeling slightly guilty about the deaths. Well, that's fine by me. But if you think I'm going to let you go after a grieving widower with absolutely no hard evidence whatsoever, you must be bloody well insane. Everything points to a tragic suicide pact by two traumatised officers. That's what happened, Broderick. Get used to it.'

Massetti strode off once more towards the front gates. Broderick stood rooted to the spot. Maybe she was right, but he'd never been an *'anything for an easy life'* sort of copper and he wasn't going to start being one now.

Broderick and Sullivan pulled up at the edge of Gibraltar's Eastern Beach, a swathe of golden sand running for several hundred metres on the eastern side of the isthmus connecting the Rock to Spain. It was well known for being Gib's sunniest beach and today was no exception. It was one-thirty p.m. and the sun was high in the cloudless sky. The beach was busy with families and those enjoying the time offered by an old-fashioned siesta to sunbathe and swim in the warm Mediterranean waters. Broderick wiped the sweat from his brow as a patrol car pulled up beside them. He was not a lover of sunshine and positively hated the beach. The open air and sunbathing were not Broderick's cup of tea. He comforted himself that his dark and ruddy cheeked complexion was entirely due to his genes and a love of fine rioja.

Walking on sand in laced up shoes was a particularly unpleasant and arduous chore, but one Broderick now had to brace himself for. Nodding to Sullivan to follow him, both detectives walked towards the water's edge, where Martin Tavares was standing, rod in hand, fishing.

'Mr Tavares?' Broderick enquired. 'I'm Chief Inspector Broderick. This is DS Sullivan.'

'What do you want?' Tavares asked, concentrating his attention on the line in front of him.

'We need to ask you a few questions about the death of PC Bryant.'

'What about it?'

'And the subsequent death of PC Ferra.' Tavares turned sharply to them — a look of genuine surprise upon his face.

'He's dead too?'

'Yes.'

'Well, well, well.' A few moments' silence passed before Tavares decided to put down his fishing rod.

Sullivan could see that her boss was suffering from the direct heat of the early afternoon sun. She, on the other hand, was glad to get out of the office and was making a mental note to get across to the beach later in the day for a swim and a little R and R.

Martin Tavares dragged heavily on a cigarette. 'So what? Ferra top himself as well, then? Or did he die from natural causes?'

'We haven't come to the conclusion that these deaths were the result of suicide, Mr Tavares,' Broderick responded. Tavares smiled.

'Well, it seems pretty obvious to me. Clearly the bastards had more of a conscience than I gave them credit for.'

'There are certain inconsistencies in both cases which are troubling us,' Broderick countered.

'Such as?'

'Well, that's for us to know at the moment, sir. Would you tell us where you were on the morning of the twelfth and the evening of the fifteenth of this month?'

Tavares now glared at them. 'Do you think I had something to do with this? Are you out of your tiny minds?'

'If you'd just answer the question, please, sir,' Sullivan insisted.

'Go to hell!'

Broderick said nothing, but glanced over his shoulder to the two uniformed constables standing a discreet distance away. Within moments they had moved in to arrest Martin Tavares.

Chapter 13

THE INTERVIEW ROOM door slammed shut behind Broderick and Sullivan. Calbot was waiting for them outside.

'Any joy?' he asked.

'No,' Broderick replied. 'Says he was out night fishing on those dates. On his own.'

'Been camping out on the beach,' Sullivan added. 'Says he needed to get away from well-meaning friends and relatives.'

'Anyone corroborate that?' Calbot asked.

'Not as yet.'

'So, motive and opportunity. Not looking great for him, is it?'

'We still need to place Tavares at the scene,' Broderick pointed out. 'Laytham's re-examining the pathology. Sullivan, you go and check with him. The forensic boys are back at Bryant's apartment. Let's see if we can get any late pickings there.'

Sullivan spoke up. 'And Tavares, sir?'

'Let him stew.'

Twenty minutes later Sullivan was at the hospital looking for Laytham. The corridors in the basement of the large building seemed endless to Sullivan as she made her way through numerous sets of double doors. Approaching yet another set, the doors burst open to reveal David Green wheeling an empty wheelchair. He moved on swiftly, ignoring her.

Glancing through the porthole windows in the doors, Sullivan could see no signs for the pathology department, just a continuation of the interminably long corridor. Sullivan had to admit that she was lost.

'Where's a policeman when you need one?' she murmured, and continued on her way.

Across town, Broderick and Calbot stepped over the police tape into Bryant's apartment, where the forensics team were hard at work. An elderly woman approached the pair.

'I told this lot it's just as you left it,' she informed them. 'Bloody nuisance, all this fuss.'

'Excuse me? Who are you, exactly?' Broderick asked.

'Mrs Sedina. I rent out the apartment. Well, not for much longer, I suppose. No-one's going to be interested in renting a place where someone's just topped themselves.'

'What a tragedy for you, Mrs Sedina,' Broderick remarked.

'But you think it might be murder now, do you?'

'Just re-examining the scene for possible new insights, Mrs Sedina.'

'Well, that's not going to help me rent it out, is it? I don't know,' she said, with a raise of her heavy shoulders and the over-projection of someone who was used to not being listened to.

'First he hangs himself, now he's been murdered. Why does everything always happen to me?!'

♦

A further series of labyrinthine corridors finally led Sullivan to Professor Laytham's office. With a gentle knock on the door, she entered and found the room empty. As she turned to leave, a set of framed photographs on the wall caught her eye.

She had never imagined Laytham to be a sporting sort of fellow, yet here he was in various athletic guises. Canoeing, parachuting, mountaineering. The picture of him holding a pick-axe atop a snow-covered mountain seemed to her a particularly intrepid shot.

'The Eiger, 1989.' Laytham's voice startled Sullivan. Turning round, she found the kindly faced pathologist standing in the doorway behind her. 'Nearly lost a toe to frostbite. Managed to hack myself to the top, though.'

'Impressive.'

'Not really,' Laytham remarked, lighting his pipe. Sullivan knew that smoking was prohibited within the hospital environs, but thought it best not to mention it to the avuncular pathologist. Besides, she liked the aroma.

'Sheer bloody lunacy, really,' Laytham continued. 'Makes you feel alive.' His eyes lit up momentarily as he said the last word. Not one he got to use that often in his line of work, Sullivan imagined. 'You indulge in the sport yourself?' Laytham asked.

'Dabble. I'm more a gym and swim sort of girl than an Alps hound. I've got a terrible head for heights, anyway.'

'That's impressive enough for me.' Laytham replied. 'Nearly killed myself on a running machine once. Slipped right off the end of it. You need guts to take on your average leisure centre these days.'

Sullivan laughed. 'Agreed. I work on a cross-trainer that's like something out of a mediaeval torture chamber.'

Laytham strolled across the office and handed Sullivan a folder from his desk.

'Nothing new here on re-examination, I'm afraid. Whatever Broderick may be brewing up, they both died from the result of hanging. Self-inflicted, in my opinion.'

'Right. Well, thank you, Professor.'

'Look, I hope you don't think this unprofessional... but as a fellow fitness fanatic, would you care for dinner sometime this week? We could exchange stories of peaks and troughs.'

Sullivan's face could not hide her surprise at the invitation.

'Well, I, erm...'

'Tomorrow night's good for me. I could swing by the nick and pick you up, if you like.'

'Tomorrow?'

'About eight, then? Now, if you'll excuse me, I've got a decapitated air conditioning salesman to attend to.'

Sullivan could find no words to reply.

'Hey ho,' Laytham added, marching off towards his cadaver-laden slab.

Broderick and Calbot exited Bryant's flat by way of the kitchen door and surveyed the scene in the communal yard.

'So, if this is now a possible murder scene, bets are he or she entered the apartment from here?' Broderick observed. 'This back door was unlocked. Maybe Bryant kept it that way, or...?

Broderick lifted up a couple of small plant pots by the side of the door. The second pot revealed a key beneath it. 'Heh. Not much of a challenge for anyone looking to get in.'

'If the door was locked in the first place, guv.'

'Exactly.'

The pair moved across the yard to a wooden door which opened onto a dark and narrow passageway running along the side of the apartment building.

'The killer would have got in and out through here, I suppose,' Broderick observed, looking at the gate itself.

'Hello, what's this?' Calbot asked, nodding for his boss to come closer. Both could now see a small piece of blue cloth caught on the lock on the side of the door.

'Wool,' Broderick suggested. 'Part of a jacket or something.'

Broderick now took in the whole door. His eye fixed on a nail protruding from higher up.

'This nail? Looks like dried blood to me.'

'It's been over a week, guv.'

'Doesn't matter. Weather's been dry.' Broderick studied the nail a little closer. 'Yes, that's definitely blood. Must have cut himself when he caught his jacket.' Broderick turned back to look at the apartment, his mind racing.

'So, our killer thought he had all the time in the world in there, then the fire alarm goes off and Bryant's landlady comes a-knocking. Had to make a quick getaway. Snags his jacket or whatever on the side door here, cuts himself and then…? Broderick now swung open the door and the pair entered the narrow passageway.'…the killer runs out here and down to the street.'

'Jumps into his car or onto a motorbike and is away.'

'Or legs it. Check all the CCTV in the immediate area. See what they throw up.'

Calbot had returned to the side door to look once again at the blood stain.

'You know, guv, if this is blood, I'm betting it belongs to Martin Tavares.'

'Only one way to find out, Calbot. Let's get forensics out here.'

CHAPTER 14

THE MARINA BAR was buzzing that evening as Sullivan recounted her rendezvous with Professor Laytham to her fellow officer.

'What am I supposed to do, Calbot?'

'Well, do you fancy him?' Calbot asked facetiously.

'What do you think?' Sullivan snapped back.

'Well, I think he's quite well-preserved for a granddad. Maybe you like 'em posh, eh?' Calbot quipped. 'Maybe a silver fox is just to the senorita's taste, si?'

''Oh, you're hilarious, aren't you? For all you know, I might not like men at all.'

Calbot's face dropped at this.

'You're not, are you?'

'Not what?' Sullivan asked in wide eyed innocence.

'Not gay, I mean, if you were...are...well, that's cool with me. I mean that would be great. Not a problem...your choice etc...'

Sullivan looked at her colleague pityingly.

'You're gabbling, Calbot.'

'Sorry, I just didn't see that one coming,' Calbot stammered.

'As it happens, I'm not gay, Calbot. But if I were, I'm sure it would be a great comfort for me to know that you'd wholeheartedly approve. Very modern of you.'

'Oh, for God's sake!' Calbot exclaimed and took a much needed swig from his bottle of Sol.

'But as for Laytham.' Sullivan smiled. 'I just don't want to hurt his feelings. He is a sort of work colleague, after all.' Sullivan stood and looked down at her young companion. 'And let's face it, men can get so unreasonable if they feel rejected, can't they? Good night, Calbot.'

With that, Sullivan left the table. Calbot watched her as she strode purposefully across the bar. If her last comment had in any way been aimed at him, she'd been wrong. This particular man felt neither unreasonable nor rejected. Just a little miffed.

At Police HQ, Broderick had decided to stay on and work late. Although he had a lot of work to catch up on, he could feel his eyelids drooping as he fought to stay awake. The ringing of the telephone jolted him back to consciousness. He picked it up.

'Broderick. Uh-huh. Yeah, put her through.' Broderick looked at his watch. He had known it would be his sister. 'You alright, Cath? Yeah, I'm sorry. Lost track of time completely. Girls all right? Yeah, okay. I'm on my way.'

He'd barely left the office, when Sergeant Aldarino appeared at the top of the staircase in front of him.

'Sir?'

'What is it, Aldarino?'

'Sorry, sir,' the sergeant continued. 'Could you stop off in South District? There's been a request for CID. Woman found dead at home. I wouldn't normally ask, sir, but we're really overstretched.'

'And it just so happens to be on my way home?'

The sergeant smiled in mock innocence.

'Hadn't crossed my mind, sir.'

Broderick sighed heavily. 'Right. Where do I go?'

Broderick's car came to a halt in the driveway of The Captain's House. He had passed the old building, with its distinctive statuesque lions, many times over the years but had never stepped foot beyond its gates. Behind them, an ambulance stood on the driveway and at the front door a police constable directed the Chief Inspector into the house as two paramedics headed out.

Inside, the small crumpled form of an elderly woman lay in a dislocated heap at the bottom of the central staircase that dominated the main entrance hall. Uniformed officer Sergeant Anna D'Angelo moved to greet Broderick.

'Weren't expecting *you*, sir,' the sergeant said.

'Apparently we're overstretched.'

'That'll be everyone watching the Man U v Porto match, sir.'

'That explains things,' Broderick replied.

'Quite an important game actually, sir. If Porto win tonight, they go on to...'

'Yes, yes, yes,' Broderick interrupted. 'You are obviously mistaking me for someone who gives a flying fart about a lot of overpaid hooligans knocking balls into nets.'

'If you say so, sir.'

'Not that I'm bitter, you understand.' Broderick managed a slight smile, realising that he had perhaps been a little too vociferous in his condemnation of the so-called 'beautiful game'. His attention returned to the case in hand.

'Fell down the stairs, by the looks of it.' He offered, crossing to the body and kneeling down for closer inspection.

'Looks that way, sir, but I'm not totally convinced.'

'Oh aye?' Broderick queried, hoping beyond hope that she was wrong.

'The medics have pronounced her dead. I just wanted a second opinion about what to do next.'

D'Angelo kneeled down on the other side of the body and pointed to a thick layer of dust on the floor beside the corpse. 'What do you make of this, sir?.'

Although not immediately obvious, a scrawled message had been left in the dust. It read simply, *'Help him'*.

'Well it would appear she didn't die straight away. That's the first thing.'

'Odd though. Why would she write it?'

'I've no idea.' Broderick replied, in all honesty. 'What I do know is, I don't give a bollock who's playing football tonight — get the CSI unit and Laytham up here right now.'

The Barbary Sports Bar roared with excitement as the referee shook his head vigorously on the large HD screen.

'Sodding penalty, ref! Any day of the week!' one of the many cries from the assembled throng rang out.

Through the din, Calbot nearly missed his mobile ringing. He recognised the number immediately. On the screen the referee had begun handing out red cards to protesting footballers. By the time order on the pitch had been restored, Calbot was outside the bar awaiting a lift from an RGP patrol car.

Ten minutes later, Calbot arrived at The Captain's House. Attempting to disguise his mild inebriation, he walked carefully towards Broderick who was waiting by the staircase of the main hall. Standing over the old lady's body, Laytham was about his business as preparations to remove the corpse got underway.

'Ah, Calbot. You must be thrilled to be here,' Broderick welcomed.

'DS Sullivan here by any chance, guv?'

'No, no. Thought I'd let her off this one,' Broderick replied.

'She won't be bothered. She's a Liverpool supporter,' Calbot moaned. Broderick continued.

'The dead woman's name is Evelyn Brooks. Widow, late seventies and I'm afraid I have absolutely no idea what soccer team she supported.'

Calbot looked down at the old woman whose death had caused him to miss his beloved Manchester United's UEFA Euro Cup challenge. His selfish thoughts were interrupted by Broderick.

'Lived here for the best part of forty-odd years, apparently.'

'Not a house I'd be keen to live in, sir,' Sergeant D'Angelo interrupted.

'Not a lover of the colonial style, Sergeant?'

'No, the style's great.' D'Angelo continued. 'Worth a fortune. No, I meant because of what happened with the Gregson murder here in the sixties. Place gives me the creeps.'

'Before my time,' Calbot muttered.

'Quite famous, actually,' the sergeant continued. 'Local solicitor. Murdered his wife, caused a sensation. Old Mrs Brooks here was a relation. After the solicitor topped himself whilst awaiting trial, she inherited the house and moved into it with her husband.

Legend has it the murderer's ghost can be heard at night calling for his wife.'

'All very interesting, but ghouls apart, did the unfortunate Mrs Brooks here fall from the top of these stairs or was she pushed?' Broderick speculated. 'Let's start by finding out who the 'he' in that scrawled message is and why she considered it necessary for him to receive help.' Broderick turned to Calbot. 'Let's start next door.'

'Sir?'

'Neighbours, Calbot.'

'What about them?'

Broderick pointed to the view of the house next door through the hall window.

'Their lights are on, Calbot. Which is more than can be said about yours. Come on.'

Broderick set off across the hall towards the front door.

'Broderick one - Calbot nil,' the detective constable muttered under his breath.

'You knew both Mrs Brooks and her late husband well, Mr and Mrs Constantine?' Broderick asked the elderly couple sitting before him in their sitting room. He had been surprised at how different the inside of the neighbours' house looked, compared to the style and tasteful opulence of The Captain's House next door. All here was modern and functional. This imposed style was at odds with the original interior design that the Victorian villa - from the outside - still remained.

'Not really, I'm afraid,' replied the husband. 'We've lived here for twenty-two years and in all that time I can remember just a handful of conversations.'

'Usually about the weather,' Mrs Constantine added. 'It's awful, isn't it?' she continued. 'Poor dear. How did she...?'

'Did her husband's death three years ago make her any more... accessible?'

'Less so, if anything. She kept herself very much to herself,' the woman continued.

'Fiercely independent, I suppose,' her husband chipped in.

'No close relatives or friends that you were aware of?' Broderick enquired.

'Well, we would usually have said no...' Mrs Constantine began.

'But?' Broderick pushed.

'Well, these last few months I noticed that someone seemed to be staying at the house. On and off. A gentleman.'

'Never saw him myself,' Mr Constantine added sceptically.

'Oh, I did, dear,' she continued. 'From a distance, you understand. Never saw his face.'

'Any idea who he might have been?' asked Broderick.

'As it happens, I think I do. I met Mrs Brooks in Marks and Spencer's last week. Quite unexpectedly, actually.'

'Go on.'

'I told her that she was looking well and she thanked me and for some reason I mentioned her visitor. She became quite agitated. Then she clammed up. But I have a theory.'

'I'm afraid my wife is a little too fond of Miss Marple, Inspector,' Mr Constantine added with raised eyebrows. Mrs Constantine continued unabashed.

'Just after Mrs Brook's husband passed away, I had a conversation with her housekeeper. Just outside the house here, actually. Naturally I enquired after her employer and she told me that she seemed to be coping alright, but was concerned to try and make contact with her only living relative. She explained that it was the Gregson boy. You know the story, I take it?'

Broderick nodded. 'Please continue.'

'Well, they had adopted the lad after the unpleasant deaths of the boy's parents in the 1960's and had lost track of him over the years. Families are strange, aren't they? Anyway, Mrs Brooks was rather keen to track him down. Understandable, I suppose.'

'And?' Broderick continued.

'Well, that's who I think her visitor may have been. Just a guess, but you did ask.'

'News to me!' Mr Constantine exclaimed.

'I did tell you, dear. Only you never really listen.'

'Charming. Isn't that just charming?'

Mr Constantine folded his arms by way of cutting himself off from further conversation.

'Poor man,' his wife continued. 'What a terrible shock this will be for him.'

CHAPTER 15

BRODERICK AND MASSETTI parked up and got out of their respective cars at the front of police headquarters. Unable to avoid each other, they walked side by side towards the entrance of the building.

'You look terrible, Broderick,' his superior observed.

'Cheers. That's what being up all night can do for a boy's complexion.'

'Your daughter? The youngest one?'

Broderick knew that by 'youngest one' Massetti had really meant the 'Down's Syndrome one'. It never ceased to amaze Broderick the lengths to which people would go to avoid actually naming the condition. Ignorance and embarrassment still lingered on in these supposedly more enlightened times.

'Daisy. My youngest daughter is called Daisy, ma'am, and she's probably been out clubbing all night with a new boyfriend. Not that I'd know, of course, because some of us had to pull an all-nighter. Old lady found dead in suspicious circumstances up on Trafalgar Road.'

'I would have thought you had enough on your plate, Chief Inspector.'

'One might have thought that, ma'am, but truth is I didn't quite get out of the building quick enough last night.'

'A dedicated officer to the end, Broderick. That's why you are so indispensable.'

The pair entered the building and continued to the Chief Super's office in silence. Once there, Massetti began to question Broderick about developments in the case that were foremost on her mind.

'When will full forensics be back on Bryant and Ferra?'

'When they're back, ma'am.' Massetti glared at Broderick. 'The lab's rushing them through as it is.'

'Well, keep the pressure up, Broderick,' Massetti insisted. 'The Commissioner is, to say the very least, concerned that we tie this one up as soon as possible. Which means yesterday. Understood?'

Broderick nodded.

'Very clear, ma'am.'

Massetti sailed on.

'The press are having a field day. The story's even playing in the UK and Spain.'

'I'm sure it is,' Broderick replied. Massetti paused for a moment.

'By the by. How's Sullivan shaping up?'

'No complaints,' Broderick answered.

'The slightest indication that she's not up to the mark, I want to know. She's only supposed to be here on secondment. You're asking a lot of her. Remember, she's here because she cocked up on a case over there. I don't want her doing the same on my piece of rock. Understand?'

'Crystal, ma'am.'

'Good.'

Broderick decided to take his chance.

'Ma'am, I need to request more resources. With both...'

His plea was cut off in mid-sentence by the ringing of Massetti's phone. The mobile was at her ear in a moment.

'Massetti. Yep, okay. Put him through. Ah, good morning, sir. I trust you're well.' Massetti waved Broderick away. As he left Massetti's office, he found Sullivan and Calbot waiting for him.

'Heard you had a busy night, sir,' Sullivan remarked somewhat archly.

'Yes. Thanks for your concern Sullivan,' Broderick replied. 'It means so much to me that you care. Calbot brought you up to date I hope?'

'He did indeed, sir. United 2, Porto 1.'

'How very amusing, Sullivan, I meant of course, Mrs Brooks' death. Firstly, check out the history of the Gregson murder up at The Captain's House. I need everything you can find on it and the whereabouts of the Gregson boy, if he's still alive.'

'On it, sir,' Calbot confirmed.

'Second priority — a mug of tea and a bacon sarnie if you can find the time between jokes, Sullivan?'

'Yes, sir,' Sullivan answered, none too happily. 'Understood.'

Sullivan, with bacon sarnies in hand, and Calbot, with the forensics results, entered the office through doors on opposing sides of the room. It was like a poorly rehearsed parody of a spaghetti western.

'Forensics are back from Ferra's, guv,' Calbot said, firing the first shot.

'And?' muttered Broderick.

'The rope's the same make as the one that hung Bryant, sir.'

Broderick's face lit up. 'Good! Excellent!'

'But... not a make that's been available for about ten years. So obviously not purchased recently, therefore hard to trace.'

'Bugger. Okay, can we proceed with a little more good news, please?' Broderick enquired.

'Well, there are several sources for the blue woollen fibres that could match with the piece we found on the door. They're checking them as we speak. Apart from that, nothing much, I'm afraid. No prints. A shoe mark on the fire escape, but nothing distinctive. Oh, and a small trace of tobacco and curry powder.'

'How eclectic,' Broderick observed.

'They're analysing both.'

'And the results on the blood?'

'Later today.'

'I see,' mused Broderick. 'So it's *suddenly nothing happened*, as per usual.'

'What do we do with Tavares?' Sullivan asked, trying to move things on.

'Let him go,' Broderick replied reluctantly. 'What other choice do we have?'

David Green's car pulled up to the front of the Tavares's house. In the passenger seat, Martin Tavares sighed heavily as he spotted the gaggle of reporters and photographers waiting for them on his doorstep. Heaving himself out of the car, he headed for the house, doing his level best to ignore the throng.

'Mr Tavares? How do you feel about what's happened to you?'

'Are you an innocent man, Mr Tavares?'

Unable to take the intensity of the intrusion, Tavares snapped. 'Yes, I am innocent. I did not kill those men. The police *know* I did not kill those men, and yet they have decided to put me through more hell. My wife is dead. I ask you... how much more pain do you wish to see me and my family go through?'

With that, he went inside, leaving David on the doorstep. He too was shaking with anger.

'Happy now, are you? Got your story? What about the police, eh? They're the guilty ones. Shame on them. Shame on all of you,' David shouted, before following Martin into the house. 'Jesus Christ, the bastards.'

Martin was sat at the bottom of the stairs. His eyes were red and his face drawn. David moved to his side.

'Can I get you anything? A glass of water?'

'No,' Martin replied. 'I just need sleep.'

He stood, and started to climb the stairs.

'Please. Make sure nobody disturbs me,' he said without looking round.

'No bother. I'll be in the study if you need me.'

A minute later, with David out of sight, Tavares quietly crept back down the stairs. Moving through to the kitchen and the back door, he left the house and crossed to the garage. Entering the garage he carefully locked its door securely behind him. Inside was the covered shape of a 1960's Alfa Romeo - once his pride and joy. Removing the cover, Tavares opened its boot and rummaged for a few seconds before finding what he had come for. He gazed long and hard at the long length of rubber tubing that he now held in his hand. His trance suddenly broken, Tavares set about the solemn task he had set himself.

CHAPTER 16

SULLIVAN SAT ALONE in the office, nibbling a tasteless fruit bar and mentally devouring the information on the screen in front of her.

'Hello there!' The voice from behind took her by surprise.

'Professor Laytham!'

The pathologist stood in the doorway, smiling. It seemed to Sullivan that he had made a little more effort with his appearance than usual. A brightly checked designer shirt and light coloured chinos were not his usual style. Sullivan wasn't entirely convinced that it was working for the prof.

'Don't look so surprised,' Laytham replied. 'My work does bring me to these parts, you know.'

'Sorry, I was miles away. Got a lot to catch up on.'

'So I hear. Pity you can't make tonight. You chaps do enjoy burning the midnight oil, don't you? Mind you, there has to come a time when 'all work and no play'... Well, you know the rest. How about tomorrow?'

'Er...if I can get away.' Sullivan lied.

'Excellent! Why don't you drop by the hospital when you're finished? That way, I can continue working in the unfortunate circumstance of you having to cancel once again,' he chuckled. 'See you when I see you.'

'Uh, sure,' Sullivan replied, as Laytham headed off. Shaking her head with disbelief, she rose from her chair. Laytham was a nice man, she thought, but somehow she couldn't quite see herself ever dating a last chance trendy. In fact, she couldn't really see herself dating anyone at all. Relationships had often been a torturous source of anxiety for her. Always preferring her own company, Sullivan had become increasingly resigned to the fact that it was just as well she did.

Her thoughts were broken by Broderick returning from lunch. He was eating a chocolate muffin. Sullivan raised an eyebrow.

'Stops me reaching for a cigarette,' Broderick announced with his mouth full. 'Confectionary. The default position of the non-smoking, stressed out professional.'

'I've given up both,' Sullivan smiled grimly.

'Congratulations. You'll no doubt live a long life.'

'I doubt it,' Sullivan replied. 'It'll just seem longer.'

Their double act was suddenly interrupted by a breathless Calbot striding into the room with a printed email in his hand.

'Guv. Gerald Gregson, only child, aged ten at the time of his mother's murder. Orphaned by his father's subsequent suicide. Only family were the Brooks, it seems.'

'How close?' Broderick asked.

'Cousins. Very distant ones at that. They inherited the house and moved out from the UK. They adopted Gerald and then packed him off to school back England.'

'How very 'of the time',' Broderick mused.

'Not a happy bunny it seems. He was expelled from a succession of boarding schools during his teens. All claiming difficulties with him. Left school at sixteen and effectively vanished off the radar. It seems the Brooks never saw him again. There's no record of Gregson ever returning to Gibraltar, and Mr and Mrs Brooks never again visited England.'

'So if her message in the dust was a plea to help him, where did it come from? Guilt?'

'Maybe,' replied Sullivan.

'And if he was Mrs Brooks' house guest, then he's been visiting Gibraltar under another name.'

'Do you think there's any chance he'll still be here, guv?'

'Unlikely. Still, we need to find him if we can.'

'With no physical description and no known name for him, that's going to be fun,' Calbot observed.

'You said you could do the job when you wrote in, Calbot,' Broderick teased. 'Meanwhile, I'll go and kick some arse over at the Glee Club.'

Broderick's exterior disdain for the forensic department in reality hid a deep respect for their work. He knew that good forensics was mostly responsible for all successful convictions in murder cases. Advances in forensic techniques and the wonders of DNA tracing had revolutionised detection work during his years as police officer. At times he resented the smugness of the scientific arm of the force, but he couldn't deny its effectiveness in identifying killers. Even if it at times took longer to get answers out of them than he would have liked.

'We're moving on this as swiftly as we can, I assure you.' Richard Kemp wasn't a man to be rushed. Not that it ever stopped Broderick trying it on anyway.

'By swift, you mean when exactly?'

Kemp, refusing to be drawn, simply continued with his work.

'The fibres are a woollen weave. Dark blue jacket or coat, I'd say. Samples from both scenes match exactly. The curry powder is a basic mix. Good quality, though. Possibly brought over from Morocco, but that's just a guess, I'm afraid. The tobacco is most probably Dutch. Aromatic.'

'Popular brand?' Broderick asked.

'Well, definitely not a 'Condor Moment'. I'd say it's a rarer shag. Oh, and I just received this note before you came in... It appears that things are happening rather swiftly. The blood results.'

'And?' Broderick asked impatiently, barely believing that Kemp had kept that information until the end.

'Not a match with Martin Tavares, I'm afraid.'

'You're certain?'

'As certain as any member of the Glee Club can be, Chief Inspector.'

Kemp turned to Broderick, a slightly confrontational look in his eye. Broderick was certainly taken aback. 'Ah,' was all he could manage.

'Yes, we've heard your nickname for us up here,' Kemp said, cocking his head to one side.

'Well, it's, uh... it's just a bit of fun, Kemp,' Broderick explained.

'A little explanation would be appreciated,' The scientist insisted.

'I don't know...it's just that you all look a bit the same, I suppose. Like members of a choir - or Glee Club - I suppose. You all seem a bit...you know...?'

Kemp was enjoying seeing Broderick struggle.

'Might it be, Chief Inspector, that you feel we sometimes 'show off' a bit? What with our incredible skills and hugely successful results and all? Do we upset you in much the same way as the squeaky clean and cloyingly perfect cast of the similarly named television programme 'Glee' most probably does?'

'I wouldn't go quite that far.' Broderick was now beginning to perspire.

'So you have watched the programme, I take it?' Kemp continued.

'I've seen glimpses. My daughters like it.'

'So I'm approaching the right neighbourhood? Am I not?' Kemp queried.

'Sort of. It's just a joke you know,' Broderick replied gruffly.

Kemp saved his most withering look till last.

'How very amusing. Anyway, the blood still doesn't match.'

'Right.'

'Goodbye, Chief Inspector.'

Broderick turned and left the laboratory, feeling like a naughty schoolboy.

'Bollocks,' he murmured.

David Green had been sitting in the small study of the Tavares's home, trying desperately to clear his mind. But instead of calm descending upon him, a new anxiety entered his thoughts. He could not explain the reason that led him to leave the study and climb the stairs towards Martin Tavares's bedroom. He would just check on his brother-in-law, he thought, to make sure he was asleep. He knew that he was not to bother him, but some nagging and inexplicable feeling was forcing him to make sure all was well.

He reached the door to the bedroom and knocked gently.

'Martin?'

No answer. Opening the door, David could see straight away

that the room was empty. Turning to check the other rooms and the bathroom, David called once more.

'Martin!'

Again there was no answer and no sign of his brother-in-law anywhere. David started to panic. Moving downstairs now, he entered the kitchen. The back door was slightly ajar. Opening it fully, he entered the garden. There was still no sign of Martin. It was then David heard the low throb of a car engine coming from within the garage. Three strides, and he was at the garage door, frantically trying to turn the handle. It was locked.

'Martin!'

He gave himself a short run-up and attempted to shoulder-barge the door open. The hinges gave only a couple of inches, and only for a split second, but it was enough to reveal the horror of what was taking place inside.

'Shit. Martin! Martin!'

Stepping back, David kicked full-force at the door, taking it clean off its hinges.

Broderick had managed to acquire an Incident Room on the ground floor of the police HQ. Operations would now be run from there. Somewhat grudgingly, Massetti had given the nod to continue the Bryant/Ferra investigations. She'd even provided a few more officers to work it. Sullivan sat listening to her boss, while Calbot worked the phone and data bases in pursuit of Gerald Gregson. It appeared that for now, Sullivan was going to be working both cases.

'So basically, that means it's not Martin Tavares,' Broderick explained. 'At least not on his own. Check and cross-check anyone who might have had a grudge against these officers, starting with the brother-in-law.'

'David Green?' Sullivan asked.

'Well, he's been as upset as anyone over this. Where does he work?'

'At St. Bernard's Hospital,' Sullivan explained. 'He's a porter. He was there when they brought Jennifer Tavares in.'

At that moment, the door to the ops room opened and Sergeant Aldarino entered with a flushed look on his face.

'Sorry to interrupt, sir. It's Martin Tavares. He's tried to kill himself.'

CHAPTER 17

DOCTOR BUDRANI AND Broderick stood in the corridor leading to the A&E department of the hospital. Budrani exuded the air of gravitas that most doctors perfect as part of their medical training. Sullivan and Calbot stood a respectable distance away, allowing Broderick to take the brunt of the news.

'Mr Tavares was fortunate to have been discovered when he was, Chief Inspector. A few more minutes and he would most definitely have been dead. As it is, he's suffering from severe carbon monoxide poisoning.'

'Can I see him?'

'Oh no, he's far too weak for that.' 'But he'll be okay?' Broderick enquired. 'There, uh, might be some long-term effects,' Budrani answered.

'Like what?'

'Well, it's hard to tell. Some forms of neurological or psychological abnormalities may develop. These can take time to present, so very difficult to pinpoint. He's got age on his side, but he did fall unconscious whilst breathing the fumes, so that will increase the likelihood of developing delayed symptoms.'

'So he's going to be a vegetable?'

'Oh, no, I shouldn't say so. It's possible that short-term memory loss, amnesia, even dementia may result. Physically speaking, there may be the possibility of some speech abnormalities due to the oxygen starvation, but it really is far too early to tell.'

'Christ, that bad?'

'Well, the fire service detected just over nine thousand parts per million of carbon monoxide in the cockpit of the car. Put it this way — six thousand will see you dead within twenty minutes, twelve thousand within three minutes.'

'So his brother-in-law really did save his life at the eleventh hour.'

'Eleventh hour, fifty-ninth minute, fifty-ninth second, if you ask me,' Budrani concluded.

'Tavares's brother-in-law came in with him, apparently. Where is David Green?'

'No idea,' Dr Budrani replied. 'Said he was going to contact family and friends.'

'Right,' said Broderick, turning to address Calbot and Sullivan. 'Can you two...?'

Broderick realised that only Calbot now stood in attendance.

'Where's Sullivan?' he questioned.

'Probably gone for a waz, guv,' Calbot replied crudely.

'*Powder her nose* would have done the job, Calbot. Humour me. I'm an old-fashioned sort of chap.'

'If you say so, sir.'

Broderick took off down the corridor.

'Come with me,' he called back to Calbot. 'We need to find David Green.'

The real reason for Sullivan's disappearance had not been a call of nature. With that evening's impending 'date' lying heavily on her mind, and having asked Calbot to cover for her, she had taken the opportunity to head downstairs to pathology. The time had come to let Laytham know that, romantically speaking, things were definitely a 'no go'.

Finding the department a little more easily than on her previous attempt, she arrived at the Cutting Room. Glancing through the portholes of the door, she could see the pathologist hard at work. Tiptoeing past, she entered the professor's office. Finding a piece of paper and a pen on his desk, Sullivan resolved to take the coward's way out and write him a note.

'Ah-ha. Making good your escape, Detective Sergeant Sullivan?'

Sullivan perceptibly jumped with surprise. The professor stood in the doorway, wearing his full surgical gown.

'Jesus Christ, Laytham!' Sullivan blurted out.

'Sorry, I certainly didn't mean to make you jump. Is everything all right?'

Sullivan composed herself. She realised how furtive she must look, but knew she had to somehow bite the bullet.

'Fine. I was... just leaving you a little note. I'm sorry, but I'll probably not manage to get away tonight.'

'Well, you've certainly gone out of your way to tell me. A text message would have sufficed.'

'Ah, well I was over here anyway. Thought it was the least I could do, really.'

'Oh? Visiting the hospital?' Laytham asked.

'Some enquiries. About the Bryant-Ferra case.'

Laytham smiled. 'Ah, yes. I'm working on your Mrs Brooks right now. Quite a mess. Old bones fracture so easily. I'll be finished shortly, though, if you fancy hanging around.'

'Uh... no, I think I'd better help Chief Inspector Broderick. Thanks all the same.'

'Right. Well, I'll call you tomorrow, Detective Sergeant.'

Laytham returned to the Cutting Room, leaving Sullivan to wonder why she had failed so miserably in her attempt to give the professor the brush off.

'Mr Green's an excellent worker, Inspector,' the General Manager explained to Broderick as they stood in the main reception area of the hospital.

'Hugely over-qualified, actually,' she continued. 'He took early retirement from the civil service and decided to devote his time to the hospital. He's also a leading fundraiser for our building fund. The fact is, in a rather short space of time, David's become quite indispensable.'

'That's very commendable,' Broderick replied.

'His sister's death came as a huge shock to him, though. They were very, very close.'

'Yes, I believe so,' Broderick confirmed.

The manager continued.

'I made some enquiries and his colleagues tell me they are a little concerned about him. He's become somewhat withdrawn. To be expected, I suppose. I've let him know that we don't expect him to come into work until he feels absolutely fully able to do so. He won't hear of it, though.'

The more the Chief Inspector heard about David Green's state of mind, the more worried he became.

'I see. Well, when you see him, tell him I need to speak with him urgently, will you?'

The hospital manager nodded and left as Calbot approached at speed.

'Sir? No sign of Green in the workplace. He's here somewhere, but no one can find him. They'll call us if he turns up.'

'Right,' replied Broderick. 'Well, no point wasting time. Let's see if Laytham has anything on Mrs Brooks.'

Down on the lower ground floor, the seemingly endless corridors all looked the same to Sullivan. Even the sparse signs that did exist gave no help, giving directions to departments she wasn't convinced she could pronounce, let alone find. She had not seen the most important sign, which clearly stated that she was about to enter a 'CLOSED' section of the hospital. But her mind had been on other things. Thinking ahead. That was about to change.

Becoming more and more exasperated, she finally opted to turn left. More double doors followed by more corridors. Suddenly she heard an unfamiliar sound. A distinct creak. She turned to see what was behind her. Nothing. Walking forward a few steps, she became acutely aware of a second pair of footsteps, but where? Why was she feeling so disorientated? Why, in a busy hospital, was it so deserted down there? She heard the footsteps again. Were they in front of her? Behind her?

She picked up her pace and headed through the next set of double doors. No corridor — this was a large room. An old operating theatre, perhaps? It was poorly lit and ominously cold. She turned to leave, but the room was suddenly thrust into darkness.

'Okay... who's there?' she called out, her voice tightening. 'If this is some sort of joke...'

Sullivan barely had time to register the noise behind her, as an arm grabbed her around the neck and a surgical pad was placed over her mouth and nose. Her momentary struggle was followed by a descent into further darkness, and deep unconsciousness.

Calbot and Broderick had reached the lower ground floor and were making their way to Pathology. A way down the corridor ahead, a porter pushed a trolley across a corridor junction, and on through double doors to the side. Broderick's first thought was that it might be Green, but although they could not see a face, the momentary glimpse of the porter showed him to have a considerably larger frame than that of their suspect. The policemen continued on their way.

'Another one bites the dust,' Calbot remarked.

'Yeah, they have a habit of doing that in hospitals,' Broderick replied.

On reaching the Pathology Cutting Room, both officers could see that nobody was at work there. Moving on to Laytham's office, Broderick opened the door to find nobody home there either. Laytham's desk was immaculately laid out. Everything in its place — pens, notepad, spare pipe and desk clock — arranged in the perfect order becoming of a surgeon. But lying abandoned on the floor by the professor's desk was a piece of note paper. Reaching down to pick it up, Broderick easily read the message and the name of its author.

'What the hell's this?' Broderick asked, turning to Calbot.

'You tell me, guv,' Calbot replied.

'It appears to be a note to Laytham from Sullivan.'

'Ah...yes...right,' Calbot muttered.

Broderick stared at his detective constable.

'Do you have any idea what this is about, Calbot?' he demanded.

'Well, not really. Only that she, er, said she was going to see him. Tell him she couldn't meet him tonight.'

'Meet him? Meet Laytham? How long's this been going on?' An incredulous Broderick asked.

'It hasn't been *going on*, guv. She's been trying to shake him off. He's a bit of a letch on the side.' Calbot was cut off by the sound of his mobile phone barking. 'Shit.'

'What?' questioned Broderick.

'Shouldn't be on in here, should it. It's a hospital — might interfere with the patients' machines and stuff.'

'Jesus, Calbot. We're in the pathology department! It'll take more than your crappy ringtone to upset the bodies lying around down here.'

'Yeah, good point,' Calbot replied as he answered the call. 'Calbot. Yeah... right... what's it called again? Okay, thanks.'

Ending the call, he turned once more to Broderick.

'That was Kemp, guv. They've sourced the tobacco. Dutch brand called Dollsberg. Not available in shops over here, you have to order it online.'

'Dollsberg?' Broderick interrupted. 'That's what he said...'

'Dear God.' Broderick froze, momentarily stunned.

'What, guv?'

Broderick quickly moved to Laytham's desk and picked something up from beside the telephone. It was a large colourfully designed pouch of tobacco.

'Dollsberg, Calbot! That's the brand of tobacco Laytham smokes!'

'That's a coincidence, guv,' Calbot replied blandly.

'Is it, Calbot? Is it really?'

Broderick's eyes now darted about the room. They settled on a door which obviously led to a large cupboard. Broderick was at the door in a moment, turning the door handle. It was locked. Taking out his pocket knife, Broderick crouched and picked the lock.

'Where did you learn to do that?' Calbot asked.

'Zumba class,' replied Broderick. The lock gave. 'Ah-ha, got it.'

The cupboard door opened to reveal a plethora of bound files and folders. A black hold-all caught Broderick's eye, and he leaned in to open the zip. Reaching inside, his hand met a large coil of climbing rope. Both he and Calbot recognised it on sight.

'Jesus, guv,' Calbot exclaimed. 'I just don't bloody well believe this.'

Broderick moved to the cupboard door. Hanging from a hook was a scarf and a blue quilted jacket. He swiftly checked the sleeves of the jacket, before turning to show Calbot what he had found.

'Look! There's a tear.'

'Guv, will you tell me what's going on?'

'The coat, Calbot! It's Laytham's! It's torn on the sleeve. Laytham is a pipe smoker — his brand of choice is Dollsberg. We have particles of that tobacco at the scene of both Bryant and Ferra's deaths. The rope in that hold-all looks pretty bloody familiar to me as well, and if you check the photos of the professor's mountaineering expeditions on his wall through there, it seems he knows how to bloody use it.'

'Wait, are you saying...?'

'On the morning of Bryant's death, Laytham turned up with a plaster on his forehead, remember? Said he'd slipped in the bath.'

'Yes!' Calbot said, realisation slowly dawning on him. 'Or cut his head on a nail on side door running from Bryant's apartment.'

'He was also wearing this jacket.'

'Jesus.'

'Not only that. That smell of disinfectant present at both scenes... it was driving me crazy, remember? I know now why it was so familiar. Stick your head in Laytham's Cutting Room, and you'll recognise it too.'

'But why? Why would Laytham want to...?' Calbot stammered.

'I don't know, but we need to find out fast.' Another thought suddenly hit Broderick.

'And where the bloody hell's Sullivan?'

The sun beating down on Broderick's head in the hospital car park did nothing to alleviate the many stressful thoughts that were firing through his mind.

'Laytham's only been on the Rock eight or nine months, Calbot. I want to know where he was before. I want to know everything about him, and I need to know now. Understood?'

'Yes, guv. Sullivan's not answering her mobile.'

'Right. Organise a search of the hospital and its grounds. Did you get Laytham's home address?'

'Sir,' Calbot replied, handing Broderick the sheet of paper.

'Right, that's where I'll be.'

Broderick opened his car door and got in. Neither he nor Calbot had noticed the dark green Peugeot estate drive by them a few moments before. If they had, they might have recognised its driver and discovered the unconscious body, wrapped in hospital bed linen and covered in a tarpaulin sheet, that lay in the back of the innocuous-looking vehicle.

Five minutes later Broderick drove past the Victoria Sports Stadium and turned right onto Devil's Tower Road. The address Calbot had given him was an apartment on the east side of the Rock overlooking Catalan Bay. His police radio crackled and buzzed feverishly as Broderick managed to escape the heavier traffic and put his foot down.

'DC Calbot reports search underway at the hospital, sir,' Sergeant Aldarino said over the radio.

'Tell Calbot to join me at Laytham's house straight away. Oh, and bring back up.'

'Yes sir,' came the response.

CHAPTER 18

CONSCIOUSNESS STARTED TO return to Sullivan in small waves as she was carried up the stairs and placed on a large four poster bed. She was aware of someone thrusting open a window, allowing a warm breeze to flutter the net curtains. She knew she should be afraid, fearful, but she was not. Her head swam with images from her childhood. Her mother and father on a beach on holiday - smiling and laughing. Her pet dog, Bruce, running along a country lane. A Christmas tree, heavy with lights and glitter. All benign. No threat at all.

Somewhere far off, the sound of jazz. Gentle syncopation, easing Sullivan back into a warm and comforting unconsciousness.

'Hey, what's going on?' the neighbour called out to Broderick, in response to the vast number of flashing blue lights and assembled police officers gathered outside the exclusive apartment building overlooking the sandy beach of the bay.

Broderick, who had been knocking on the door of apartment number seven, turned to answer.

'Police. I'm looking for Professor Laytham. He lives here, I believe.'

The elderly man looked concerned. 'Yes, that's right. Gerry's okay, isn't he?'

Broderick peered through Laytham's window; the apartment looked to be deserted.

'Is he in, do you know?'

'Haven't seen him. Works at the hospital.'

Something was niggling away at the back of Broderick's mind.

'He keeps pretty irregular hours,' the man continued. 'Mind you, he's been spending quite a bit of time up at his cousin's place.'

Broderick spun round to face the man. 'And where is that?'

The man looked slightly startled at the brisk response and stuttered as he answered. 'The Captain's House, up on...'

Broderick interrupted. 'Yes. I know exactly where that is.'

'His cousin's quite elderly and lives on her own. He's been looking after her a fair bit.'

Broderick had been about to try and gain entry to the apartment, but now suddenly realised what had been nagging him. 'Wait. Did you say Gerry?'

'That's right, yes.'

A daze of realisation filled the Chief Inspector's features as he mentally began piecing things together.

'Gerry Laytham. Gerald *Gregson*!' Broderick announced.

'Has Gerry done something wrong?' the neighbour asked. But Broderick was already waving the other police officers away as he ran to his car.

Sullivan awoke. She had no idea how long she had been under since last she was conscious. The music was still playing somewhere in the distance, but a different, slower jazz number now filled her awakening senses. She immediately felt less calm and more than a little disoriented. Across the room she could see the back of a man standing by the windows. He seemed to be inspecting a large knife, which glistened in the light of the late afternoon sun. The man turned to reveal himself. Professor Gerald Laytham smiled across at her.

'Ah, welcome back, Detective Sergeant,' Laytham said softly. 'Or may I call you Tamara?'

Sullivan could not speak. Her throat was parched and her heart pounding.

'Don't rush,' Laytham advised as he walked towards her. He reached for a glass of water from the bedside table and brought it to her lips. Sullivan drank. At last she mustered speech.

'What do you want?' she asked.

'Right now I'll settle for you changing into the clothing I've arranged on the bed for you, Tamara.' He nodded towards the peach tinted boudoir robe and silk charmeuse trouser set spread out neatly beside her.

'Why are you doing this?' Sullivan murmured.

'Just do as you're told and change into the clothes. Or believe me, I will kill you where you lie.' He raised the point of the knife a little. 'Forgive me for not averting my eyes, Tamara.'

Sullivan pulled herself up to the side of the bed.

'Look, I really think...'

'Do it!' came the ordered response. Laytham's normally warm, avuncular tone had been replaced by something coldly detached and menacing.

Sullivan recognised the tone. She had interviewed psychopaths in the line of duty and Laytham was clearly in a place where reasoned argument would never reach him.

Moving slowly round the side of the bed, Sullivan looked down at the silk nightdress. Struggling to control her breathing, she slowly began to unbutton her blouse.

Across the room, Laytham poured himself a large glass of single malt scotch from a bottle on the dressing table. He then turned to watch Sullivan as she disrobed. Sullivan felt his cold intrusive stare upon her, as she delicately pulled the nightdress over naked shoulders and slipped on the silk slippers that had been laid out on the floor by the bed. Somehow she had to escape. She glanced towards the bedroom door.

'Oh, I really wouldn't contemplate it if I were you, Tamara,' Laytham said, raising his glass. 'To your very good health.' He took a sip of his drink and swallowed. Then moving closer, he stopped a few feet from Sullivan and looked up at a large picture hanging upon the wall. It was a full length portrait of an extremely glamorous woman in a scarlet dress. 'That's my mother, you know. They kept that picture hidden away up in the attic.'

'She's...' Sullivan tried to speak.

'Beautiful? Indeed she was, Tamara. Indeed she was,' Laytham mused, his eyes gazing at the picture in an almost trance-like state.

'Does she remind you of anyone?' he asked.

Sullivan looked once again at the striking portrait hanging above them. The subject of the picture gazed down at them with an imperious look. Her long, dark, curling hair tumbled over her shoulders. Her eyes were bright and her lips scarlet and full. She looked every inch a Hollywood movie star. A woman used to getting her own way. But the artist had also managed to capture something else about his subject. There was the slight look of the trapped about her. A wild animal caged.

'No.' Sullivan shook her head. 'I don't recognise her.'

'Then you should look in the mirror more often, Tamara. The moment I saw you I felt I had gone back in time. You look just like her.' Laytham smiled, as though this gave him some comfort.

Sullivan looked again, but could not see any real resemblance at all. But it was enough that Laytham had. Whatever his warped mind was seeing, she knew it would be best not to disagree with him.

'Ah, yes,' she responded. 'I can see something, now you mention it.'

Laytham stayed looking at his mother's image as if unable to break the spell it had put him under. Meanwhile, Sullivan weighed up her chances of getting to the door. She might have tried it, had her captor not suddenly downed his scotch and moved to the door himself. 'Your slippers are beside you Tamara. Slip them on, if you will.'

Sullivan looked down at the velvet embroidered slippers beside the bed. Obeying the request, she slipped her feet into them and looked once more towards Laytham.

'Shall we, Detective Sergeant?'

Sullivan hesitated for a moment, then followed her captor out onto the landing and down the large staircase that led to the main entrance hall of the house. At the bottom of the stairs, Laytham waited for her and then gently took her by the elbow to guide her through to the drawing room. It was a room that Sullivan imagined only existed in stately homes - large, imperious and like everything that was happening to her - frightening. Laytham gestured for her to sit down on the large chaise which dominated the centre of the room. Once more observing the knife in his hand, she quickly obliged. Laytham moved to a large gramophone in the corner of the room and placed a needle on the record spinning on the turntable. Once again the sound of jazz filled the air.

Sullivan was now drawing on all her reserves. She knew she had to do everything in her power not to upset Laytham. One false move and he might lose it and lash out. Staying calm and engaging him in conversation offered her the best opportunity of gaining time and achieving escape.

She watched as Laytham moved slowly across the room towards her. As he reached the back of the chaise, he leaned over to touch her hair. If his knife had not also appeared just inches from Sullivan's throat, she might have taken her chances there and then. Although Laytham was a big man, Sullivan had deduced that she stood as good a chance as any of tackling him successfully. She also guessed that Laytham had figured this out too and was taking no chances.

As Laytham continued to stroke his prisoner's hair, the room suddenly exploded around them. It was the sound of splintering wood and breaking glass caused by the main door to the hall and the French windows being burst open with terrific force. Several police officers led by Broderick and Calbot stormed into the room, stopping abruptly at the sight before them.

With practised speed, Laytham had grabbed Sullivan around the neck, holding the blade of his knife inches from her throat. Broderick immediately waved for his fellow officers to stand further back. Both he and Laytham stared into each other's eyes.

'Oh, you're a little early, Inspector Broderick,' Laytham said, showing no hint of panic or emotion. 'I'd hoped to have finished my work here before you arrived.'

'Put the knife down, Laytham,' ordered Broderick. 'Let her go.'

'I'd love to oblige, old chap, but I'm afraid no can do. Please feel free to change the record.'

Broderick nodded to Calbot and watched him move over to the gramophone and stop the record in its tracks.

'Nice house your cousin had here,' Broderick said.

'Evelyn? Oh, yes. Had to do her post-mortem this afternoon. Least I could do for her, really.'

'Useful, that. Being the pathologist in charge of your own murder victims,' Broderick observed.

'Oh, yes!' Laytham smiled. 'It's come in rather handy, I must say.'

'Bryant? Ferra? I take your late cousin as a given, of course.'

'Oh, no. She was an unfortunate, not to say inconvenient accident. Stupid woman must have taken a tumble. Nothing to do with me.'

'She wrote 'help him' in the dust beside her before she died. I presume she was referring to you, Gerry.'

'Oh, how sweet. Pure remorse, I'm sure. Pity she and her husband couldn't have been a little more understanding when I was younger. But I suppose that was because of the shame.'

'The shame of your father's conviction?' Broderick asked.

'That and the fact that he hung himself,' Laytham replied. 'Not the done thing for a pillar of the community, is it? The murder happened in here, you know. In this room. My mother. Stabbed with a knife. In many ways not dissimilar to the one I'm holding to your colleague's throat at this very moment, Inspector.'

'Leave her be, Laytham,' Calbot pleaded. 'Please.' Laytham laughed.

'And why should I do that? I think my feelings about the police are fairly clear by now. It was you and those like you who took my father away from me in the first place.'

The police inspector leans over the woman's body. The boy cannot bear to look. A trickle of blood falls down her cheek, a final crimson animation from her lifeless body.

He clings helplessly to his father as the policemen lead him from the room. Another policeman holds the boy back and pushes him to the ground. The breeze is warm, the room hot. But inside — deep inside —the boy feels cold.

'And that's why you murdered Bryant and Ferra?' Broderick stepped forward half a pace. 'Because the police took your father away from you?'

'Bryant, Ferra…and the rest of them,' he replied.

'Rest?' enquired Broderick.

'Oh dear me, yes. I'm not entirely sure how many. It's become a bit of a habit over time. Always the same — make it look like suicide. Make sure I'm the pathologist on call. Make sure I get away with it.'

'Until now?' Broderick questioned.

'A little sloppy, I agree, but perhaps that's because I really don't much care anymore. About anything. Least of all about death. Which I suppose makes me an even more dangerous proposition to you, Chief Inspector.'

Broderick moved an inch closer to Laytham, treading very carefully indeed. 'Why did your father murder your mother, Gerald?'

'She was a whore! Cheated on him. Constantly.' The anger burst from Laytham, turning his face ugly and distorted. Broderick attempted to calm him once more.

'Please. Let's stop this, Laytham,' he entreated. 'Let DS Sullivan go.'

No sooner had the words been spoken than Laytham's grip on Sullivan tightened. Broderick backed away.

'All right. All right.'

'I'll stop this soon enough, Chief Inspector. But not before a little swansong. *As it began, so shall it end.*' Laytham smiled enigmatically.

'What do you mean?' Broderick asked.

'My father worshipped me, you know. As I worshipped him. He was a truly good man, you know, Broderick. My mother cheated on him with just about anyone she could, including that bastard police officer who took my father away from me that day.'

'He knew? About her affairs?'

'He had the patience of a saint. I suppose he accepted it because he loved me. But I never could, you see. I couldn't accept that my mother was nothing but a cheap whore.'

Suddenly Broderick could see clearly. He knew what had happened.

'It was you, wasn't it?' Broderick asked simply. 'It was you who killed your mother.'

Laytham smiled. 'I suppose moments like this are why you get paid the money, my dear Broderick. Of course I did. I hated her. I hated her almost as much as I loved my father. And, oh, my father loved me. He loved me so much he was willing to sacrifice himself for a murder I had committed. To save my reputation. To give me a life. Such knowledge can drive a person insane, you know. Which, I fear, is what it may have done to me.'

'We can sort this out,' Broderick pleaded. 'Just let Tamara go. Please let her go, Gerald.'

Laytham said nothing, but dragged Sullivan to her feet and

retreated to the library room door and out into the hall, all the while checking that no police were in his immediate vicinity.

'Don't, Laytham! Please!' Calbot yelled.

Again, Laytham said nothing. With a maniacal grin on his face, Laytham shoved Sullivan to the ground, moved to the kitchen door and took off.

Broderick and Calbot were at Sullivan's side in an instant.

'Sullivan, are you okay?' Broderick asked first.

She looked up at him, her eyes on fire.

'I'm fine, guv. Just get the bastard!'

CHAPTER 19

THE SIDE OF the house had an overgrown garden path running up beyond the three levels of terraced garden to a gateway on higher ground. Through the gateway there appeared to be a narrow and still more overgrown pathway which rose up the side of the Rock itself. It was, in fact, a natural shelf that had been developed in the 1860s to allow access to a viewing point some fifty metres above. Landslips and erosion had meant that it had been declared unfit for use in the late 1940s, but Laytham had climbed it often as a boy. It had been his secret escape, his hideaway from the tensions and coldness of his home. He stood now at the gate, a length of rope in his hand. Behind him Broderick and Calbot, followed by several uniformed officers, were approaching at speed.

'Coming to watch, Inspector?' Laytham shouted back to them. 'Very brave of you! Didn't think you'd have the stomach!'

The police officers followed him upwards. Thirty metres on, Laytham was forced to climb over a dishevelled barrier which crossed the climbing path. A discoloured sign on it read; 'DANGER. DO NOT PASS'. Beyond the barrier, the path became a much more dangerous proposition. Narrowing, as the sheer drop to its side increased, it was clear why nobody had thought to venture up it for many years. Eighty metres further up, Laytham reached a small outcrop. Turning to check that he had time, he began to tie one end of the rope around the stump of an old tree which half-protruded over the edge of the outcrop. As he made good the knot, he turned to see Broderick and his fellow officers finally catching up with him.

'What the hell are you playing at, Laytham?' Broderick yelled.

'Attempting an execution, old boy! One that's long overdue,' Laytham replied, tying a noose in the free end of the rope.

'Don't you think that's the coward's way out? You need help, Gerald. This isn't the answer,' Broderick pleaded.

'Oh, but it is. You think I did it because of the pain? The rejection? Because my mummy didn't love me? Oh, no, no, no. I did it for pleasure, Inspector. Pure pleasure.' He smiled as he spoke. 'Oh yes, I left that bit out, didn't I? Watching people die. In pain. In agony. It's not the same when they come to me to be cut up. They've gone. They're nothing. Just rotting flesh and bone. I killed my mother because I enjoyed it, Gus old son. And for that, by law, I am guilty.'

Laytham moved to the very edge of the outcrop and looked down over the sheer drop below.

'I think I have the requisite drop. Don't you, Chief Inspector?'

As he spoke, the ledge beneath Laytham's feet began to crumble. Unable to fall backwards to safety, Laytham was propelled forward and over the edge. He began to hurtle through space, the noose of the rope tightening around his wrist, checking his fall as the rope brutally yanked hard and taught. The sound of Laytham's arm being ripped from its socket and the terrifying scream that emitted from his throat chilled those above, watching.

'Get help! Anything!' Calbot yelled across to the police officers behind him.

'No time,' Broderick yelled. 'Stay over there. The path won't take your weight.'

'Sir, be careful!' Calbot shouted back.

Broderick moved forward, kneeling down on the outcrop and reaching forward to get some sort of grip on the rope. At last he achieved his aim and began the surely impossible task of pulling the hanging man back up to safety. Below him, Laytham's screams and pitiful cries of pain pierced the air. Lying on his stomach now, Broderick managed to get another hand to the rope and began to pull in earnest.

Bit by bit, inch by inch Broderick heaved heavily on the slippery rope. Each pull brought a new scream of pain from below, but there was no help for it. For a short while Broderick persuaded himself that his actions might actually save the life of the cruel and callous psychopath at the other end of the rope's length. But then reality kicked in. To his right, Broderick noticed that the roots of the tree stump that was securing the line were beginning to come loose from the ground. Upping his efforts to superhuman levels, Broderick realised that he was fighting a losing battle. Even though he could now see Laytham hanging just a few metres below, time was running out. The professor was looking up in utter desperation. This was the worst possible end for a controlling, meticulous psychopath. An endgame that Laytham could not control and dominate to his final breath.

Suddenly another hand grabbed the rope. Sullivan was at Broderick's side.

'Get the hell back' he yelled at her.

'Is that an order, sir?' Sullivan yelled back, grim determination on her face. 'Dying down there is too easy for that bastard.'

Looking over at the sheer drop, Broderick knew that there was no way he would be able to pull Laytham up by himself. And Sullivan was right. Dying like this was an easy escape for the vile creature at the end of the rope.'

'No, Sullivan,' he yelled back into her face. 'That is not a bloody order!'

Tightening their grip on the rope, both officers began to pull with as much power as they could gather. By inches, managing to haul the screaming man back up towards the ledge. Laytham was just feet from safety when both officers heard a terrifying crack. Behind them the tree stump had snapped free of its roots, losing its hold upon the rock face. The line began to slip out of control through Sullivan and Broderick's now bleeding hands. Below them, Laytham saw what was about to happen and started to reach out in even greater panic. His eyes bulged with a fury and disbelief that his grande finale should have been so outrageously stolen from him. With his dislocated shoulder and broken arm giving his body a grotesque and twisted shape, Laytham once more screamed with the pain of a wild animal caught in a trap. Nothing could now stop the force of gravity as it propelled his wretched body downwards to its painful fate on the rocks below. Broderick and Sullivan looked helplessly on as the psychopath fell screaming to his painful, ignominious end.

'May God have mercy on your soul!' Sullivan whispered under her breath.

Realising how close they'd both come to experiencing a similar fate, Broderick called across the narrow, crumbling pathway to Calbot on the far side.

'Calbot? I think we're going to need some help getting back from here.'

CHAPTER 20

CALBOT AND BRODERICK stood on the side lawn of the Captain's House. It had taken some time to get everyone down from the perilously dangerous ledge high on the Rock behind them. Both detectives glanced across the garden to where Sullivan was being checked over in a waiting ambulance.

'We couldn't stop her, guv.' Calbot explained. 'Followed us up there in a bloody dressing gown, for god sake. First thing I knew, she'd moved past me and jumped over the gap in the path. Nutcase. Brave as hell, but still a bloody nutcase.'

Broderick stood in silence. A warm evening breeze ruffled his hair as he took in the view over Gibraltar Town and out across the Straits of Gibraltar. It was the time of evening when the setting sun seems to fill the western sky completely. A bright burning orb, falling ever quicker to the horizon and colouring the distant mountains of Morocco a deep crimson red.

'I suppose you could say that hanging was too good for him, guv,' Calbot continued..

'You might also say that the punishment fitted the crime. How's Sullivan?'

Sullivan sat on the back of the ambulance, a paramedic bandaging her hand. The silk trouser set and robe she had been forced to wear, was torn in several places and one of her slippers had been lost.

'Looking pretty good to me.' Calbot smiled. 'Not much keeps her down.'

'Yes... she's... a good officer,' Broderick added thoughtfully.

'You okay, sir?' Calbot asked, not used to the sound of compliments coming from his boss's mouth.

'Course I am. Why wouldn't I be?'

Leaving Calbot behind, Broderick headed across the lawn towards the ambulance.

'That was a close thing, sergeant,' Broderick informed his detective sergeant.

'Yes, sir. Well timed by you, if I may say so.'

'Kept your head pretty well. Both down here and up there on the rock face.'

'Do you mean *pretty well... for a woman*, sir?'

'No, Sullivan. I mean pretty well for a *police officer*.'

'Thank you, guv.'

'All the same, don't go wearing that Marlene Dietrich outfit to work tomorrow.'

'At least I didn't have to disobey an order.'

'No. Chief Superintendent Massetti will be delighted about that.'

'And you, guv?'

'I've always been a bit of a *means to an end* man myself. Just don't make a bloody habit of it Sullivan. Okay?'

Sullivan smiled and turned to look at the old house, now empty of life.

'Well, this place has seen enough tragedy in its time,'

'Not least the tragedy of Laytham's...I mean *Gregson's* delusion.'

Sullivan looked at her boss.

'He got it all wrong, you see.'

'I don't understand, guv.'

'Gregson thought his father loved him and that his mother had made his father suffer. But I've read the full report from the archives which included his father's statement after arrest. I also made a few enquiries elsewhere. It seems that Gregson Senior was the big philanderer. He was a well-known womaniser here on the Rock. Treated his wife very poorly, by all accounts. Gregson's mother eventually began to take retaliation on him by having her own lovers. The young boy was only privy to his mother's behaviour. His father carried on his affairs elsewhere.'

'But to have your father carry the can for a murder you yourself committed? That must have been what turned Gregson into a madman.'

'Yes, he truly believed that his father had sacrificed himself so that he, the son, could live without blame. However, the man's statement suggests another story. Gregson knew it was his son that had killed his wife and, according to his statement, didn't hesitate in offering the police that information. One line of that statement has stayed with me. He said, *'Don't think that boy isn't capable of murder. He is a calculating brat and should never be trusted. It wasn't me. It was him.'* Not exactly the words of a loving father wishing to protect his only child.'

'Dear God.'

'The police dismissed his version out of hand. So, Gregson's father hung himself, not to protect his son, but to avoid the shame and disgrace of being judged guilty himself.'

'Why didn't you tell him when you had the chance?' Sullivan asked.

'Gregson had a knife at your throat. I thought it best not to aggravate him further. The truth for him, you see, may well have been more horrific than the fantasy.'

Sullivan took a moment for this to sink in. Broderick thought it time to change the subject.

'So, at the end of your first couple of weeks on the Rock, do you have any observations, assistance or advice you'd care to give me?'

'Come to think of it, one of each, sir. I observe that your collar is twisted at the back, so I'll *assist* you by straightening it out,' she said, smiling as she did so. 'And my advice would be to go home and pour yourself a large scotch.'

'And to think you came all the way from London just to tell me that. Almost a waste of valuable police resources.'

'Oh, that's just for starters, sir. I can waste a lot more than that.'

Taking no notice of the comment, Broderick moved off across the lawn to his parked Mercedes. Sullivan watched him go. Without looking back, Broderick called to her.

'You need a lift, Detective Sergeant?'

'Yes, please, guv,' a surprised Sullivan answered, gathering the rest of her clothes

'Well, get a bloody move on, then!'

Sullivan smiled to herself and looked up at the Rock towering high above her. It had been there for a million years and more, but tonight, as she crossed the lawn of The Captain's House to Broderick's waiting car, that simple fact gave her an unexpected and much needed sense of comfort.

THE ROCK

If you've enjoyed this Sullivan and Broderick murder investigation, please sign up to robertdaws.net for news about the next novel, Killing Rock, plus free offers and competitions. Also, a free download of Tunnel Vision – a Sullivan and Broderick ghost story. Thank you.

THE ROCK

ALSO AVAILABLE

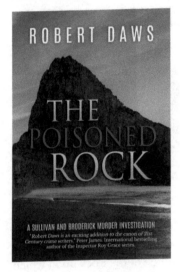

£8.99

ISBN 978-1911331216

URBANE PUBLICATIONS

In London, the British Government has declassified a large number of top secret files regarding British Military Intelligence operations during World War Two. One file, concerning espionage operations on Gibraltar, has been smuggled out of the U.K. to Spain. It contains information that will draw Sullivan and Broderick into the dark and treacherous world of wartime Gibraltar. A place where saboteurs and espionage plots abounded. Where double and triple agents from Britain, Germany and Spain were at war in a treacherous and deadly game of undercover operations. It is only a matter of time before past and present collide and a dangerous battle begins to conceal the truth about the Rock's poisonous wartime history. Detectives Sullivan and Broderick become caught in a tangled web of intrigue and murder that will once again test their skills and working relationship to the very limit.

ACKNOWLEDGMENTS

I have been fortunate enough to be a yearly visitor to Gibraltar for some twenty-three years. The warmth and spirit of its people, together with the wonder and magnitude of the Rock upon which they live, has never ceased to amaze me. Even as I write, I am looking forward to my next visit.

I would like to thank those within the Metropolitan Police Service and the Royal Gibraltar Police Force who have given their time to offer help and guidance. It has been invaluable. Also to Mr Stuart Green, Press Attache to the Gibraltar Government and my friends at the marvellous Gibraltar Tourist Service.

I hope I will be forgiven for playing hard and fast with the internal geography of the Gibraltar Police H.Q, as well as Gibraltar's main General Hospital, St. Bernards. I have also changed the names of several places and establishments. Other than that, I have tried to be as accurate as possible with situation and location.

Thanks also to Adam Croft for his knowledge and enthusiasm for books, writing, pubs and fine ales.

To Ted Robbins for access to his huge brain and endless enthusiasm.

Matthew Smith at Urbane Publications. Wise words and support from a terrific publishing mind.

Huge thanks to my agent at Independent, the great Paul Stevens, for years and years of help, energy and kindness.

For Betsy, May and Ben for being lovely and remaining only mildly interested in what I do.

Last, but not least, to my wife Amy, for her wisdom, patience and wonderfully creative mind. A dear writer friend, Christopher Matthew once wrote, 'Eighty-five percent of a writer's life is spent thinking and thinking *very hard*. Unfortunately for writers, unless they are seen to be pounding away at a laptop keyboard, nobody really thinks they are working at all'. Amy has always understood this strange process, even when my 'thinking' has drifted into a pleasant little afternoon siesta.

ROBERT DAWS

As an actor, Robert Daws has appeared in leading roles in a number of award-winning and long-running British television series, including Jeeves and Wooster, Casualty, The House of Eliott, Outside Edge, Roger Roger, Sword of Honour, Take A Girl Like You, Doc Martin, New Tricks, Midsomer Murders, Rock and Chips, The Royal, Death in Paradise, Father Brown and Poldark. He has recently completed filming a second visit to Midsomer Murders and will shortly begin work on the film, An Unkind Word.

His recent work for the stage includes the national tours of Michael Frayn's Alarms and Excursions, and David Harrower's Blackbird. In the West End, he has recently appeared as Dr John Watson in The Secret of Sherlock Holmes, Geoffrey Hammond in Public Property, Jim Hacker in Yes, Prime Minister and John Betjeman in Summoned by Betjeman. He is returning to the stage in 2017 in Alan Ayckbourn's classic comedy, How The Other Half Loves.

His many BBC radio performances include Arthur Lowe in Dear Arthur, Love John, Ronnie Barker in Goodnight from Him and Chief Inspector Trueman in Trueman and Riley, the long-running police detective series he co-created with writer Brian B Thompson.

Robert's third Sullivan and Broderick novel – Killing Rock – will be published in 2017, as will his thriller, Progeny. His first novella, The Rock, has been optioned and is being developed for television. He is currently co-adapting the international bestseller, Her Last Tomorrow, by Adam Croft for television, as well as writing a new thriller for the stage with award winning television and stage writer, Richard Harris.

Urbane Publications is dedicated to
developing new author voices, and publishing
fiction and non-fiction that challenges, thrills and
fascinates.

From page-turning novels to innovative
reference books, our goal is to publish what
YOU want to read.

Find out more at
urbanepublications.com